INNOCENT

BEINGS

(BE THEIR VOICE)

By Barbara Thumann-Calderaro

Printed in the United States of America

First Printing, 2014, Second Printing, 2015

ISBN 978-1-63192-434-7

Book Baby Publishing

ACKNOWLEDGEMENTS

No one walks alone on the journey of life; just where do you start to thank those who joined you, walked beside you and helped you along the way?

INNOCENT BEINGS (be their voice) would not have been possible without the support and encouragement of my husband of 32 years, Vincent Calderaro. Thank you dear, for cleaning up the dinner dishes and not missing me (too much) while I spent countless hours on the computer at night. Thank you for making copies ("one last time") and for patiently answering all my, "How does this sound?" questions about the farm. And for being one of my final eyes for the finished manuscript.

Thank you to my daughters, Amanda and Emily, for their understanding and for giving up their computer time so I could finish, "just one more paragraph."

Thank you to Gene Baur, the founder and author of *Farm Sanctuary,* who enlightened me to write my first story after his lecture at his book signing in the spring of 2012 in Clifton, NJ.

Thank you, Kip Anderson for producing the eye-opening documentary, *Cowspiracy*. It was my pleasure to have met you.

I'd like to also thank all the animals who inspired me to make them a little more human by giving them a voice - that I hope many people will hear. Some of my characters, based on the lives of the animals who peacefully live at Farm Sanctuary and the Woodstock Sanctuary, have had their names changed (to protect their privacy, of course).

Words cannot express my gratitude to my editors Erica Martinez (now a vegetarian), Heather Sowalla at Windy Hills Editing, Rebecca Josephsen and (my aunt) Cathy Fernandez for their professional advice and assistance in polishing my manuscript.

I also wish to thank personally the following people for their contributions to my inspiration, knowledge, and other help in creating this book:

My brother, Harry Thumann (a vegan), who would throw snippets of "hard to hear" information about where our "food" came from (*during* mealtime!)

before I realized how the animals traveled to reach their destination – my plate.

For my relatives and friends, especially my first readers: (my mom) Carole Thumann, my dearest lifelong friend, Janet Thompson Ford, and George Thompson for giving me the encouragement to keep writing.

Thank you to my friends: Steven DeVito, Rose Zembryski, Margit Smith, Mike Robson and Phillip Kim. Their simple question of, "How's the book coming?" truly encouraged me and made me happier than they knew.

For my friend: Debi Eustis (a vegan), who at times *became* the voice of the animals and would personally thank me and encourage me on my first writing project.

Thank you to my friends with whom I have dined these past two years. Your compassionate choice of not eating meat while with me was noticed and appreciated.

I'd also like to thank Vladislav Golunov, the founder of "Freakin' News," and the artist, Ray Gregory, for allowing me to use the "moo-ving" cow picture that is on the cover.

INNOCENT BEINGS (be their voice)

TABLE OF CONTENTS

INNOCENT BEINGS (be their voice)

PROLOGUE

**"If you light a lamp for somebody, it will also brighten
your own path."**

~Buddha

Ok, I'll admit I'm not usually so *zenny* in the wee
hours of the morning, especially while walking alone
in a dark forest, but these philosophical quotes have
been popping into my mind ever since I left my
house. It could be from the combination of being in
the mountains and the high altitude; my lack of sleep
and a need for a second cup of caffeinated tea; or
possibly the reason is that I've recently learned some
unsettling information. Someone (could you believe a
stranger no less?) lit my responsibility light and made

me realize that my lifelong food choices were all wrong – immoral!

It all started a few weeks ago on my way into the city. Let me explain: I was sitting on the train, minding my own business, when a leaflet was shoved in front of my face. I didn't respond at first (It's a known rule living in the New York City area that you don't speak or make eye contact with people you don't know — especially extremely rude ones!) and I disregarded my intruder by turning my head and waving my hand that I wasn't interested. Although, I did manage to get a quick glimpse of what he was peddling and noticed that there were pictures of cute puppies and kittens on the cover. The animals were so precious that they would probably make a criminal pause for a moment or two and say, "Awww." Maybe leaflet-guy wanted money to help stray animals I thought, or maybe he wanted me to open my bag, so he could steal my wallet. I decided it was best just to ignore him.

What caught my attention was the picture of little white puppy on the cover. It immediately brought me back to the day that we had to put our eleven-year-old dog, Lily, to sleep. It happened over a year ago, but the emotional wounds of that day are still so raw that I sometimes find myself crying at silly little memories. Lily was my birthday present when I was seven years old; we practically grew up together! People who have never had a pet have given me strange looks and said, "It was only an animal," but I loved her as if she were part of our family. She was my friend. I never thought that losing a seven-pound little fluff of love would throw me into such mourning. Oh, the tears I cried for my baby...

"Whatsamatta, you don't like animals?" the pushy leaflet-guy said to me, interrupting my thoughts; he shook the paper a little closer in my face to get my attention.

Hey, how dare he! I growled and grabbed the paper, blinking back tears in order to get a better look at this person who was now getting on my nerves.

"I love animals!" I shouted. The rumble of the train drowned out my voice, but it didn't matter; no one was there. It seemed that as soon as I took the pamphlet, this annoying guy was lost in the crowd. Moments later, the train screeched at my stop, and I shoved the leaflet into my bag, forgetting all about the incident — until a few weeks later.

I was out at the mall for the day and had decided to take a break from shopping and grab a bite to eat — a rare event since I don't enjoy eating alone. Resembling a wild animal stalking its prey, I

13

circled the food-court reading the highlights of each eatery: Black Angus burgers, glazed pork spareribs, spicy chicken wings... I even tasted a sample of sesame chicken that a young Asian woman was handing out before I made my decision. I never get a big meal at the mall, and chose a simple bacon cheeseburger and a bottle of water. I found a place to sit near the escalator, thinking that if I had something to read I would be distracted from being alone — and that's when I remembered the arrogant leaflet-guy and his adorable animals. Fated like a high school time capsule with unknown information that would change my life; I dug for my buried and forgotten treasure that was somewhere waiting to be discovered at the bottom of my bag.

I unwrapped my cheeseburger and straightened out the pamphlet. I was ready for some easy reading as I enjoyed my lunch. Maybe it was an advertisement for puppy paraphernalia. After Lily died, my family and I swore that we would never go through the hurt of losing another sweet dog again. Well, six weeks later, our Maltese puppy, Benjamin Franklin, came into our lives, and we have been spoiling him ever since. Benjamin hasn't replaced Lily — they have two very distinct personalities — but he has helped fill that void a little bit, and we do love him very much.

Sitting in the mall, I had the chance to take a better look at the cover and noticed that, *Why Eat One but Not the Other?* was captioned under the collage of precious pets. There was also a tiny picture of a pig in the corner. I took the first big bite of my meal. The saying made no sense to me at first, but then the reality of its meaning hit me: Why *do* we eat some animals but pamper the others with sweaters and toys, and love them as family members? I wiped my mouth of the bacon grease and took another bite of my cheeseburger while I started flipping through the pages. Then, I stopped chewing. I realized that this pamphlet, which I thought I was going to *enjoy*, explained all the horrors that farm animals have to endure before becoming our food. I placed my lunch on the table and spit out my mouthful of burger in my napkin. Suddenly, my food felt abnormally chewy. I put my meal aside, and self-consciously glanced at the people around me eating their lunches. I saw a couple of teenaged boys having a good time while eating hot-dogs, and a heavy man licking the bones of his baby back ribs. In the other direction, I noticed a nicely dressed, older woman trying to inconspicuously wipe the juice off her mouth as her lamb meat gyro dripped. And nearby, under the golden arches, sat a young mother coaxing her preschooler to eat another chicken nugget. "Come on Steven, eat your meat. It'll make you a strong boy," she said as she waved the tiny plastic toy in his face. I remembered that I'd shouted, "I love animals!" to the leaflet-guy. And, I *do* love animals — all animals! I looked up at the eatery menus again and imagined I read: mouthwatering pulled-poodle sandwich, crunchy kittens on a bun, homemade soup of the day: collie noodle! What…EWW! I gagged loudly, and quickly scrunched up the rest of my cheeseburger in its wrapper. I continued flipping through my pamphlet, but I didn't want to read it anymore. It was like watching a horror movie by covering only one eye; I couldn't stop!

Ten minutes later, and without going into disgusting details, I ran to the bathroom and threw up my half-eaten cheeseburger. Needless to say, I haven't had meat since.

Looking back at it now, I find it ironic that I was handed life-changing information from a mysterious stranger on the subway in New York City and had my dietary "aha" moment while my head was in the toilet at a mall in Paramus, New Jersey. So now, as a newly determined vegetarian, I'm struggling with the disturbing realization of the truth of the matter in regard to animals, their lives, and their journeys from birth to…unfortunately, my plate. I've been trying to understand, while coping with guilt, why I remained *in the dark* for so long.

These past few weeks, I've been haunted with questions such as: Why was I mechanically comfortable eating meat all my life? Why have I never doubted my food choices before when the facts about meat could have been easily googled? I suppose the answer (as repulsive as it sounds) is both plain and simple: Animal flesh tastes good! My big juicy cheeseburgers or barbeque chicken thighs, ribs, breaded pork chops, and bacon — they *are* delicious! Chicken soup is a comfort food when you're sick and even has medicinal purposes to make you feel better, right?

And, that's not all – think about it – our culture has always accepted this meat-eating practice as the norm. Our holidays and family or community celebrations center largely on meat dishes, and the meats connected with each festivity. Our holiday ham, leg of lamb, corned beef, and Thanksgiving turkey are a main part of all celebratory occasions. Who hasn't been to an expensive party where prime rib wasn't on the menu? Also, can you seriously see your friends and family coming over to watch the big game and eating carrot sticks and arguing over a bowl of lettuce instead of devouring a mountain of buffalo wings and beefy tacos? No, I don't think so!

I'm shocked that I've never considered the animals behind beef, chicken, and pork during celebrations or my everyday meals. I've never thought, "How did this meat reach my fork or my fingertips?" Meat was purchased at the store, usually my mom cooked *it,* and then we all sat down and ate *it.* I've never put those animals in the same category as the beloved pets. I thought of meat as an *object* and called it, "it." The gruesome process of how meat is made was never discussed – or even considered. Whoever questions the animals' "Circle of Life?" It's just accepted, and, in this case - eaten.

What confuses me is meats' nutritional value? I always believed that we were *supposed* to eat meat to stay healthy. Protein, calcium, iron, and other nutrients are important ingredients for a healthy body. These "facts," engrained in all of us from a young age, became second nature so we could become responsible adults and pass them down to the next generation. Every child knows that a glass of milk or a container of yogurt is good for you.

18

"Important for strong bones," our milk-mustached heroes tell us in all the advertisements. And those cows look so happy in those pictures too! I suppose, like almost everyone else, I didn't want to know that our core belief in nutrition has been based on half-truths and lies.

Come to think of it, I never felt *right* about eating animals but never realized I had an option in the matter. When my cousins were young, I remember them asking me what kind of tree hamburgers came from. I sugarcoated the truth the best I could while fabricating little fibs such as: "That's why God made animals," and "We have to eat meat for protein and to stay strong." My goodness, I think I might have felt more comfortable explaining the facts of life to them than where meat came from!

Of course, I know that fruits and vegetables are also necessary, but can I thrive off them alone? I've heard of vegetarians all my life, and thought of them as hippies or extremists. In my mind, I've even questioned vegetarian parents' beliefs, thinking that they might have been nutritionally neglecting their children. *No milk? What are they, insane!*

Also, what do I eat and drink now for the rest of my life?

Today (weighed down by my guilt) is the first day of (being responsible for my dietary choices for) the rest of my life. I'm finally going to do something about it! I'm not exactly sure what — I'll figure that part out as the day goes on. Today, I'm *brightening my own path; I'm illuminating my mind*, and I'm...jeez, thinking too *Dalai Lamaish* again!

MY JOURNEY BEGINS

As my soul-searching journey begins at the crack of dawn on this unseasonably warm morning in November, I realize that I'm guilty of forgetting my cell phone (which I left right next to my bag, in order *not* to forget it!), as well as getting here a few hours earlier than I planned. (I didn't want others to distract me from my thoughts.) I suppose that's all beside the point right now. I'm here, I'm excited, and I'm ready to change!

I had recently read of a rescue farm called "Animal Haven" and I was determined to find out more about what I'd learned. Animal Haven, set on a natural location in a wooded part of a forest, is currently the home of many animals saved from slaughterhouses, neglect, or abuse. They now live out the rest of their natural lives in peace and protection. I can't think of a better starting point for my focus on a newer lifestyle, to change my direction for living and eating in my life.

I park my car in a pasture surrounded by an old-fashioned, split rail fence. I shine my penlight in search of the "this way" arrow. I'm going to hug a goat, pet a pig, get to know a cow or two, and play with some chickens. I hope my experience will help me think differently about eating meat. It will definitely make me feel differently about eating *them*.

As I reach a rocky path in the dim shadows of this early morning, I remember a quote that I heard recently during a church homily: *Sometimes the truth is as simple as the dawn of a new day.* However, I'm now thinking that noon would have been a better time to search for the truth.

My inner Buddha moves me to believe that the only lights guiding me this morning are the moon and my self-enlightenment of a new awareness.

My inner, and very optimistic voice, convinces me that the farm will be open ridiculously early. Of course, they'll be thrilled to have a guest and insist that I come in and relax, and have a strong cup of tea and perhaps a toasted bagel before we get started. That way, I can sit down for 15 minutes to read a few pamphlets before I start my new life. Nevertheless, right now, I'm trying to walk the walk and feel the experience of hundreds of animals who have also traveled along their life's path to this sanctuary, their new "home."

Did they *know* that they were being rescued? Could they even *comprehend* this?

Did they *feel* that a continuation of their nightmare was going to take place?

Know, comprehend, and feel — are these words even used when describing animals?

Another saying comes to mind: *All beings tremble before violence. All fear death. All love life. See yourself in others. Then whom can you hurt? What harm can you do?*

"Beings?" I say aloud, shuddering as I realize that this also might have been intended for animals.

Would people listen if the animals could *tell* their story? Would they believe? Would anything change? Can something be done?

Wouldn't that be something if I could *be* their voice? I laugh a little too loud at the thought, startling a little chipmunk staring at me from a nearby rock. Maybe I should write a story about the animals I meet today. Now that's an idea! Years ago, my fifth-grade teacher, Mrs. Smith, told me that she enjoyed reading my composition on my family's traditions, and I do enjoy writing as a hobby. I was thinking of taking a journalism class next semester in college, so this might be a great opportunity to get started!

Compassion is having the courage to change the world. I shake my head and look around, half expecting to see my brain's lost marbles on the ground. Did I read that on a T-shirt or was it a bumper sticker? I don't plan on changing the *world* — just myself. I better get some caffeine in me soon because these philosophical crazy ideas are now invading my thoughts.

Now, where is my map? I've reached a densely wooded area of the forest that I don't remember being on the farm's diagram. I balance my belongings on my bended knee and unfold my Animal Haven brochure. According to the directions, I think I might be, umm…completely lost! Twisting my head to the side, I try to make sense of my upside-down map, I decide that it looks like I might have turned "right" instead of "left" at that big oak tree. Or was it a maple? I stand up; trying to get my bearings from the location of the moon, when suddenly I get dizzy, but it's a weird dizzy, more like a spinning sensation. A cold sweat panic washes over me. I feel that someone, no, umm… something, is watching me! I hear a rustling sound and see big, beady eyes staring at me from behind a nearby tree.

Holy jeez! What is that? I grab my bag slowly, and I try to steadily walk away without causing too much of a commotion. My thought is that I don't want to startle this wild beast into attacking me. I only manage to take a few wobbly steps before the

24

creature lunges at my leg. "LEAVE ME ALONE! STOP!" I scream struggling to fight it off by kicking at it, which makes this monster cling onto me even tighter. In my fright, I think a fox? Bear? No. What kind of animal has thin arms that can grip onto me so tightly? As I stumble, I try to aim my grasp towards a cluster of branches and vines to keep myself from falling, but the branch gives way and I tumble down into a small ditch. I hear screaming. It takes me a moment to realize that the sound is coming from my own mouth. The world seems to be happening in slow motion, but I'm spiraling too fast to keep its pace. Then, as quickly as I (or was it the world?) began to spin, it stops as I whack my head into something hard. I scream again, but this time no sounds come out of my mouth. In a panic, I try yelling even louder. "_____!" Oh my goodness, why can't I speak? I can't see anything either, yet my eyes *are* open. Where am I? I don't know — it's too dark! I hear voices and I hear cries, but they don't sound — human!

What's happening to me? How am I going to get out of this ditch for help? My mother is going to be furious! She didn't want me coming here alone. I try to feel my surroundings: the damp earth, some branches, twigs…yippee — my penlight! I stop moving. I hear breathing close by — too close. Then, someone speaks:

"A VISITOR...? We have a visitor!"

I look up and see a turkey. TURKEY?! I look away. That can't be right. I rub my eyes hard, take a deep breath, and then I look again. It *is* a turkey! But, was that turkey *talking* to me! And, those eyes — they look familiar. Could it be? Were they the beady eyes that were looking at me when I fell and hit my head?! Is this turkey the monster who grabbed my leg and made me trip?

This isn't real! I laugh — but without a sound. Again, I close my eyes tight, and wish with *all* my might, for the bump-on-the-head imagination to stop playing tricks on me.

I open my eyes slowly, expecting and hoping that this talking turkey disappeared or perhaps would just gobble-gobble at me, but there she is — looking at me as if *I'm* the crazy one.

"Hello?" she says waiting for an answer. Maybe I should try pinching myself...

The pounding of my heart is echoing in my mind. I calm myself by thinking that it *is* just a dream. I did just hit my head. I am up early; I need breakfast, and I'm still tired. Yep, it's just a dream. I'll wake up in a few minutes and find someone to attend to what is obviously a brain injury. We'll all have a good laugh when I tell them I heard a turkey speak to me.

I look up to try to reply to this illusion of a talking turkey; however, only a little air comes out of my mouth. What's happened to my voice? What's happening to me?

"WELCOME TO ANIMAL HAVEN!"

"HELLO!" the turkey says again, shouting a little louder this time and peering down into the ditch at me. "And welcome to Animal Haven! What are you doing sitting there? Do you need a wing to help you up?"

I don't move. Should I reach up and take hold of her wing for help? I don't think so! Was this the creature that grabbed me and made me fall? Are turkeys dangerous? I'm sitting alone and dazed in a ditch. Can she kill me by pecking me to death?

The turkey jumps into the ditch with me, and I try to scramble away. She notices my panic, and shimmies over a bit at a comfortable safe distance away from me. I relax a little — just a little. She points to the entrance post with her wing and shrills…

"I said 'HELLO!' Why don't you come right in and we'll start your tour! We love having visitors!

I smile and nod. Did she say "Tour?" Never mind that - she spoke!

28

"VISITOR!" she shrieks again as she looks around, "Where is everyone else?

I don't answer. "Everyone else?" Huh?

She shrugs and continues, "Thanks for coming to visit us on this beautiful morning! We all have our tales to tell you! Get it? Okay, sorry, I'm talking gobbledygook, and I am out of breath! This time of the day is ideal for jogging, and I've had a few too many coffee beans for breakfast — not a good combo." She says shaking her head, which makes her wattle waddle. "I'm feeling overly caffeinated, a little higgledy-piggledy, I like to say.

"Where are my manners? I apologize for sounding like such a flibbertigibbet, but we usually don't get visitors this early in the morning. You took me by surprise with all your screaming and fluttering. I'd like to introduce myself."

The turkey slowly extends her wing for me to shake, which I awkwardly do.

"And I'm pleased to meet you, by the way. I'm so glad you're here. My name is Miss Honey. They call me that because of the color of my feathers." She continues looking around. "VISITOR...!" She screams again. "My goodness ... why can't they hear me?"

I shrug, I don't know to the turkey - to the turkey! Huh! Did I just do that? What am I thinking? A flibber…what? Am I trying to communicate with a turkey? I did just shake her hand — I mean her wing. I quickly look over my shoulder. Who is she shouting for? I try to mime that I have no voice, but she doesn't notice. In fact, it doesn't seem to matter to her anyway, she just prattles away. She appears friendly enough, but most turkeys are friendly, right? Huh? What?! I don't know any turkeys. What I do know is that on Thanksgiving, they are eaten.

I remind myself that it's obviously a dream. I hit my head and it's … but it can't be a dream because I can smell the sweet grass and the fresh earth. Can you smell in dreams? Even though it's still dark, I can see the outline of the mountains and the tall trees. I can feel the cool morning air. I can hear the crickets and the first birds of the morning as that turkey continues to speak…

"Usually, everyone is running willy-nilly around here, but it's early…before dawn. I'm guessing everyone is still sleeping since we were up late getting ready. My Romeo, I mean *the* rooster should be up soon.

"Anyway, I am the hostess," she says with a slight nod of her head. It's a perfect day for you to be

here, in fact. The excitement is quite high 'cause of
… Thanks-Living feast!" She says jumping to her
feet. "Ohhhh… tomorrow is such a SPECIAL day!
How I love Thanks-Living!" She sings while doing a
little dance, and then the turkey stops suddenly and
gives me a head-tilted look as if I didn't understand
— which I don't. "Wait, let me slow down and explain.
On Thanks-Living, all the turkeys are honored,
served like royalty, I tell ya'…"

If turkeys are served, why isn't she running out
of here? Why isn't she afraid? But, she didn't call it
"Thanksgiving," did she? Maybe it's different?

"…the works: a buffet of greens, lemon balm
pie," she continues as she ticks them off on her wing.
"…pumpkin turnovers, peaches, and other delectable
doohickeys, and, my prize recipe of mashed clover.
That's what I'm making for the feast this year - fresh
mashed clover! It is SOOOO good…"

My nerves are calming down with this, "get
attacked by a turkey, fall into a ditch, hit yourself on
the head and hear the turkey speak" condition and
I'm finally getting a chance to check this turkey out.
She looks familiar. Has she been on TV? A crime
show of some sort? No! She's plain looking, but she
makes herself look pretty by accessorizing — a bit
too much, I might add. She's wearing stone-studded

glasses, attached to an eyeglass necklace; a small scarf that sits right under her wattle, and flutters as she moves her head while she speaks; and tiny gold loop earrings. She's kind of cute looking. I could be wrong, but I think she's wearing makeup. Huh! Where was she going all dolled up like this?

Miss Honey stops talking and gives me the once over. Hey, is she checking me out?

"Yea, some of those turkeys, good birds they are, good birds. All animals are good here, and they all have a story — an animal's tail. Hehe-haha!" She flaps out of the ditch and looks at me. "Come on, let's walk, and I'll tell ya a story about the farm."

I manage to stand up, brush myself off and stretch my arms. I look down at my leg and see that it's tangled in a mass of vines. I suppose the turkey didn't attack me after all, which makes me feel a little safer. And, I guess the dizzy spell made me disoriented. Maybe I need to eat— that would explain it but...not the loss of my voice though, umm... that is strange?

I didn't realize I was sitting down for so long, and I'm a little stiff. I bang the charlie-horse feelings out of my legs before I gather my things — oh my things! It's only my backpack with a few essentials. It's turning into an old-fashioned nature weekend –

no makeup and (UGH!) no means of communication, just a little money, chapstick, the Animal Haven map, a bottle of water, a snack, and a few … but this is a dream, right? Do you have your "things" in a dream? Oh well…it looks as if I do.

I notice, from the corner of my eye, that the turkey is impatiently drumming her feathers while staring at me strangely. I smile and quickly grab my backpack. I climb up out of the ditch, and do as I'm told to do and follow her. Hey, this ditch isn't as deep as I had thought!

"Every year, Animal Haven takes in hundreds of animals who have either been abused or have escaped death while on their way to the slaughterhouse to be made into, umm … food." Miss Honey says in a serious "tour lecture" voice. "To be honest with you, that's what our lives are, were … umm … could have been - DEATH!

"These animals and the birds, good, fine folk they are — they have themselves a heart, ya know, and feelings too. It's sad…real sad," she says shaking her head. "They love their babies and they really enjoy each other's company. They amazingly don't hold grudges about how they've been treated before coming here. Sure, some of them might be a little jumpy and shy around people, and oh they miss their mamas, even though some never even really had the chance to meet mama — know her," she says as she stares right into my eyes. "Yeah, my friends here have forgiving hearts, but they don't forget. Noooo, they'll never forget." She waves her wing indicating for me to follow.

"I tell ya, their stories are gonna' break your heart, yeah, break your heart. Okay now, we have cows here, sheep, pigs, chickens, ducks, goats, geese, a couple of bunnies and my favorite — turkeys!" She adds with a silly grin.

"All of us, like I said, have been rescued in some way or another. Every so often, we'll have a 'farm rescue alert.' That's when we get many rescued animals at once. We all have to stop what we're doing and skedaddle to get ready. The welcoming committee gets out the banners, and others will make sure our new friends have a comfortable place set up for them when they get here. We all have a job to do here, ya know?"

Wait a minute! Is this chick —I mean this "turkey"— is she for real? It just dawns on me what she's saying. Did she say that they "have feelings?" They "love their babies?" They "miss their mamas?" They "have jobs?" They "have stories?!" And, they have, umm — me! What a great idea! I'm a writer

(Okay, I'm not, but I guess, deep down, I always wanted to be one, which is all beside the point at the moment), and I can interview the animals to make their stories public. I was thinking about writing a story on animals anyway. But, how can I interview with no voice? How can I...?

"...here, we have over a dozen barns and acres of pasture — 'pasture of pleasures,' we call 'em," she waves her wing in a displaying-an-item-on-a-game-show motion. "And we're happy now ... oh, so very happy," Miss Honey says smiling, "but before, some of these guys ran for their lives, or they were so sick, and some were found 'cause they were left for dead ... 'downers,' they're called."

I'll take notes! I don't need a voice to write things down. I open my backpack again. Now, where is my notebook and pen? I start rummaging through...here it is. I begin writing notes on everything Miss Honey has told me, and then I stop. This is crazy. This is really crazy! This is perfect! I smile as she continues...

"It's not a good life outside of Animal Haven. You see all those pictures on milk containers and meat ads of happy cows, and you imagine the pigs playing in the mud, baby lambs frolicking in the fields... all lies! 'Malarkey,' I say! When are human folk going to *realize* that they're all real lies? Hehe-haha! Realize... *real lies*,'" she cackles at her joke. "I shouldn't be laughing now, but, get it?" She nudges me with her wing, and then turning serious again says, "It's sad, really. It's like a scary kind of sad. These stories have sugarcoated our horrific reality of torture and slaughter! That happy animal façade, as Romeo calls it, has masked the truth to the gullible public for years."

I throw my hands up as if I surrender. What I read in that pamphlet was disturbing to me, but I frankly don't know enough to comment (not that I could) on what she's saying.

"Cage-free, no antibiotics, free-range...are all empty promises to make the human folks less guilty about eating 'happier' animal flesh. Human folk are even willing to pay more money for these fancy lies too! As we say in the birdhouse, 'I don't usually ruffle my feathers that easily,' but the lies that they're telling human folk is so they don't get disgusted and ...mad. It's a fool's paradise out there!" Miss Honey squawks, shaking her head. "They don't want human folk to know the truth about where their food comes from — or should I say, 'how?' It's totally deceitful what they tell you people, but it's not illegal. Anything can be done to an animal whose flesh, milk, or eggs that are sold. They can lie about it if they want because that's what people want to know. I've seen people close their eyes and cover their ears to the truth. Why? And, now here's the real kicker, the point is not just the cruelty and the inhumane treatment my friends have gone through to get to the end of your forks, but these people are getting sick, ya know, cancer, diabetes, obesity, and over half the people who reach the age of 85 have Alzheimer's, just from eating us! Crazy! It just doesn't make sense. It's all gobbledygook to me! Human folk, you're smarter, right?"

I nod my head up and down in agreement. Is this a rhetorical question or is she honestly asking me? Yes, we're smarter — but she doesn't seem to notice. Why is she telling me all of this? Lies? Isn't this just the way things are? People eat meat. Meat comes from animals. Then I remember that this is why I'm here. I guess that I too am guilty of closing my eyes and ears, figuratively speaking, to the facts. I had so many questions that I came to see the animals, to learn, and to do something, but I didn't know what.

"What did you say your name was again?" Miss Honey asks, interrupting my thoughts.

I try to speak again. "_____," but nothing comes out. I have an idea: I mime that I will write my answers for her.

"Your name is 'Shaky-Hands?'"

I shake my head no and grab my notebook, and I write again as I look at her. I wonder if she can read. Just because she can speak doesn't mean that she can...

"Are you an artist? Are you a writer?"

I mime "longer, stretch it out..." Oh, goodness, am I playing charades with a turkey?

"A reporter? Yeah, you're a reporter, and you're here to interview us?"

I nod my head "yes-yes-yes!" Close enough. I'll take it! I touch my nose. I try to yell "BINGO" but again, only air comes out. I guess "interviewing" the animals and writing it down is a good idea!

"Reporter?"

She notices my big smile. My name — okay, my new name — is "Reporter." I've been called worse, so this isn't so bad. I nod my head "yes."

"'Re-por-ter,' am I pronouncing it correctly?" she asks. "Okay then, I'm glad you have a name. It's a little strange, but nevertheless..."

Obviously, this turkey thinks I'm crazy! This turkey *thinks* I'm crazy. When was the last time I

thought something like that? I had wisdom teeth
pulled out years ago and the pain medicine made me
a bit delirious. No, no, no — this is different, this is …

Miss Honey puts her wing on my arm,
interrupting my thoughts again, "We're not saying,
not to eat meat, Reporter, that's your choice, but we
want human folk to know the truth, and then to make
a decision and to help us. It's upsetting, how ignorant
and nincompoopy some people can be in all walks of
life: doctors, important people, and educated people.
They forget that we are all God's critters."
Miss Honey clears her throat and tests her voice with
a "me, me, me…" before she begins,

"All God's critters got a place in the choir. Some
sing low…"
she squats and quickly steadies herself before falling
"…Some sing higher…"
she screeches on her tippy-toes,
"Some sing out loud on the telephone wires, and
some just clap their hands, or paws,"
she looks at her wings,
"or anything they got."

She nods, pleased with herself and says, "You
know, I'm not a real singer like Romeo. Have I

39

mentioned him? She asks with a shy smile. He's the farm's crooner. He's also our educated rooster here. His motto is: 'Ignorance is bliss, but when you have knowledge, you then have a responsibility.' Are you ready for some knowledge? Are you ready to be responsible? Come on let's skedaddle, lickety-split. Follow me under Animal Haven's welcome sign and off we gooo!

"We'll find your voice. Maybe it's in with the chickens," she says shrugging. "Everything ends up there. That one hen, Lora, she has a bit of a problem – but I'm not the one to talk. I do have a few more coffee beans in my pocket. Want some?"

I nod my head yes, then shake it no, and then shrug my shoulders for maybe. I mean no to the coffee beans and yes, I'm ready for knowledge. Miss Turkey seems to have lost patience with me and walks away. Where is she going? What did I just agree to? Anyway…I guess I should follow.

THE GRAVE:
IT STARTED WITH EWE

"BLAH-BLAH-BLAH. Blah-blah," Miss Honey says as she stares right into my eyes. "I don't understand human folk, and this is what I usually hear them say, but with you, I'm a little confused. Why aren't you speaking? I don't want to make it an issue but can't you say *anything*?"

I shake my head and try to yell, "'I HAVE NO IDEA WHY I AM NOT SPEAKING. I FELL, HIT MY HEAD, AND NOW I HAVE NO VOICE. I WOULD LOVE TO CHAT WITH YOU. I HAVE PLENTY OF QUESTIONS TO ASK!" Only air, a wheeze, and some spit flies out of my mouth. I mime that I lost something, and then I just shrug my shoulder.

"Don't you worry about it, Reporter. As I said before, we'll find your voice. It has to be here somewhere! I'm so happy you're here to interview us; the animals do love to talk." Miss Honey smiles sweetly, "Especially me."

"We're almost there. I don't want to start your tour all willy-nilly, so let's start at the end. The end shows how the beginning got started, after all. We're going to The Grave."

I stop walking for a second. She nudges me to move with her wing.

"No, no, no, now don't be afraid, it won't be scary or depressing at all, I promise! 'The Grave' is a good place. It's where you go after you had a good and happy life — a place of honor and remembrance.

"Come on now, it's way in the back. The moonlight will help us see. Be careful, now. I don't want you falling again."

We walk up a slight incline and she guides me around some bare bushes. I pause and start to chuckle as I get a glimpse of our moonlit shadow: me and a turkey are walking hand and wing. Suddenly, she spreads her wings to stop me. Her pace is now slow and careful. It's obvious that we have just crossed onto hallowed ground.

"Reporter, we're here, at 'The Grave,'" she says in a tone of hushed reverence. "Here is where Meryl Sheep is buried. She was the first resident at Animal Haven. Meryl was so very special. She was an important friend to the older animals here and a legend to the rest. Some say she rose from the dead after her first life. She died, the final time, after a long, peaceful life but – she died with dignity. You can't ask for better than that!" Miss Honey reasons with a tilted head, waving her wing slightly.

"See that headstone with the etching of the little lamb? Right under her birth and death dates the epitaph says: 'Meryl Sheep: saved from a stockyard, died from old age, happy, and loved. Ms. Sheep took the first step to change our minds, lives, souls, and choices.'

"The story has it that Meryl was only a few months old," Miss Honey explains while tidying up the grave. She lets out a sad sigh, "Ohhh, she knew her Mama for only a short time, most likely only for a couple of weeks, but her mama's love stayed in her heart forever. Farmer Harry saved her then…OH, Farmer Harry!" She lets out a shriek and then covers her beak with her wing looking around guiltily. "He's the one who runs this place," she whispers, "with my help of course!"

Miss Honey smiles at me as though we've known each other for years and we're sharing a story about our friend. Did she say "*Farmer* Harry?" Could he be a person? Maybe he can help me get my voice back and get me some medical help for my "hearing-a-turkey-speak" condition. I have to keep my eye open for this guy.

"It was a darn hot summer's day ..." Miss Honey begins the story as if she's told it thousands of times. She stops and looks at me to explain, "Meryl would tell us her tale as we all sat around during the Summerfeast...OH, Summerfeast!" She flaps her wings holding back her excitement. "That's a celebration of life, a real hootenanny we have here on the farm in the summertime. We party until the cows come home," then softly adds, "and sometimes even later than that, but don't tell Farmer Harry that we stay out past our curfew.

"Umm..." Miss Honey shakes her head, "where was I? Yes...Meryl. She always started her story the same theatrical way. Meryl was shy, especially around people. I heard her once say that she always wanted to be an actress, and by telling her story loudly and dramatically she felt as if she really was one. Maybe, her acting abilities also made her feel as if it weren't her life she was talking about, I'm not sure. We all have our own ways of getting over things.

"Meryl would speak clearly and powerfully, then pause to get everyone's attention. She'd wait until they were real quiet before going on.

"Did you know that sheep can read the emotions of other sheep by looking at their

44

expressions like humans? Sheep can also remember human folk and sheep faces for years. That's just a little FYI about sheep, or is that TMI for Y-O-U? Hehe-haha — just messin' with ya," Miss Honey says with a cackle and a wing nudge.

No, I didn't know sheep could do that!

I have a flashback of my favorite meal as a child: lima beans, white rice and... lamb chops! I hold back a gag thinking of Meryl and my meat. Miss Honey jolts me out of my thoughts as she loudly continues the story.

"'BIG trucks pulled up to the farm,' Meryl would say, 'the animals were panic-stricken!'

"They heard stories how the animals would leave and never come back. They knew their day was coming but, *what* could you do?" Miss Honey asks.

I shrug my shoulders and I make my best sympathetic face. I want to respond the right way. Huh? It's a turkey. A turkey is talking to me and I want to act politically correct?

"Most of the animals didn't want to leave their friends, their families, or their homes," Miss Honey says matter-of-factly with a wing wave. "Others would think it was an adventure. Some were bold, but then they obeyed after seeing the cruel treatment the animals received if they got out of line."

"'There was fear in the air that day, and the smell of *blood*.' Meryl would cry out, 'Hundreds of goats and sheep were pushed onto that truck. Some were whipped and some were even electric prodded to hurry.'

"Meryl was too young to leave, but ya know, wrong place, wrong time; she was pushed and ended up with the others. She screamed for her mama, but she never saw her mama again."

I quickly cover my mouth, after I surprisingly let out a loud sob. Now I feel a little embarrassed. I have to calm down. I notice that Miss Honey is giving me a strange look. Did she hear me? This is the second time today that I've felt embarrassed in front of a turkey. I can't make this a habit.

"They couldn't breathe because of the ventilation bein' real bad and all," she continues, "and they had no water. Meryl soon collapsed from heat exhaustion. When the doors opened up she couldn't move. Meryl would throw her head back and say, 'I passed out and dreamt of my mama. When I woke up, I was lying on a pile of dead and dying sheep, calves, and other animals that I couldn't even recognize.'

"Meryl would stop speaking for a minute," Miss Honey whispers. "It's like she could still hear those crying baby sheep and goats calling out for their mamas. She'd shake her head to get those sounds and hurtful thoughts out of her mind before she continued telling her story. She didn't want to remember, but she didn't want her story to be forgotten either, ya know?"

Miss Honey waits for my answer, so with my teary eyes I put my hand on my heart and sympathetically shake my head.

"Meryl described how the maggots were feeding on the other dead animals and the stench was like nothing she ever smelled before. She passed out again.

"Is this too much for you, Reporter? You look a little squeamish. You don't have a weak stomach, do ya?"

I shake my head 'no' as I twist my face into a knot. I can handle it, I can! What a darn shame!

Here I am, sitting at an animal graveyard in a forest while listening to a turkey telling me sad stories about a lamb, I'll wake up soon, but then I start crying. I can't help myself. She was just a baby! What about her mama? All this violence, for lamb chops! I quickly wipe my eyes and Miss Honey waits for me to calm down before she continues.

"To make a long story short, Reporter, let me just tell you that all of the animals listening to her personal story would be blubbering too, even though they knew it ended happily."

Miss Honey says, "Meryl then thought she heard voices again, human voices! She froze in terror. She thought that they were coming back to hurt her. She tried hard not to move. She heard them coming closer and closer. She couldn't make a sound. It was like even her cries for help were afraid to come out of her mouth. That's when she heard him — Farmer Harry! He sounded different – nice, like us. He had a sympathetic tone in his voice. It was hard to believe because it was such an unfamiliar concept to her. She knew right away that he had love in his heart — like her mama. She felt it. He sounded very kind *and* sad at the same time, as he looked at all the animals lying there, like garbage. It was as if he could *feel* their pain, their lives and even their deaths.

"She turned her head and their eyes locked," Miss Honey explains. "'It was as if a missing puzzle piece was finally found in both their lives. For a second, she even thought he was her mama. He was shocked to see a live animal staring at him. She gathered all her strength and cried, 'MAMA' before she saw darkness again."

I have to meet this Farmer Harry, he sounds amazing!

"Meryl would stand while telling this part of her story," Miss Honey clarifies, "as if a stage spotlight was shining on just her, and she was basking in its glow. This was her moment, and she knew it, but she wasn't hoity-toity about it. She would then laugh and laugh as all the animals applauded and jumped up and down. The little ones in the back would start to cheer, 'Farmer Harry, Farmer Harry...' Miss Honey shouts as she air punches with her wing. "Meryl was pleased to know that her life really mattered. Her legacy would go on!

"Farmer Harry didn't leave her there to die. He cared. He *cared* for a dying sheep! She couldn't even comprehend that a human could have so much love in their heart for an animal — for her! She never thought it was even possible. Meryl was just a lamb, a living animal, and she needed him."

Farmer Harry, he's the man!

"Meryl was surprised that humans were so much like sheep. Did you know that sheep have strong emotions just like humans? They can feel fright, anger, happiness, and on those long lazy days, they can even feel bored. *You* can imagine how she felt. I can't because I'm a turkey."

I wondered this, I didn't know it for sure, but I did think that animals might be able to feel — like people, but not exactly "like" people, but they must feel something, right? Dogs and cats love their owners. "Man's best friend" is his dog. I know for sure Lily loved me unconditionally. Even parakeets have ways of showing their — "feelings?"

I must have shaken my head, because Miss Honey is staring at me. I can't comprehend all this. I'll write it down in my notebook and think about it later. It is far too much for my "bump-on-the-head" brain to handle right now.

"Meryl explained she liked to think that Farmer Harry needed her just as much right then, too," Miss Honey continued. His passion for animals and helping us is something he wanted to do his whole life, and here it was—the opportunity, and here she was— needing *his* help!

"He carefully took Meryl into his van and drove her to the nearest vet. Meryl finally woke up there. The veterinarian massaged life into her little body and gave her more water. A little while later, Meryl stood up and took a step.

"Do you know why that first step was very important?" Miss Honey nudges me with her wing to answer her, and when she remembers that I can't, she continues. "If we had an animal history book, Meryl's legacy would be in it, really! Her first step was just the beginning to save hundreds of thousands of animals during her long and happy lifetime. That was the first step for Meryl *and* Farmer Harry to take together, to start Animal Haven.

"Meryl and her BSFF, her 'best sheep friend forever,' used to sit in our 'pasture of pleasures' and knit little blankets from their own wool for the new babies at Animal Haven. They knew these babies would need something to comfort them after losing their mamas, and they wanted to welcome them to their new home. Meryl believed that she could never do enough to thank Farmer Harry for her second chance in life.

"We don't use the wool from the sheep after they are sheared here. And the sheep on the outside…," Miss Honey grimaces while shaking her head disapprovingly. "You know the ones where you get the wool for your pretty little sweaters and all those poor animals have a horrible life! They are bred to have more skin and more wool and because, umm … their parts…umm, down yonder, get a little

51

yucky, their skin is sliced off without any painkillers. Isn't that called mutilation?"

I gasp as I cover my mouth and nod — yes, that is mutilation! I didn't know. I didn't know! I think of my nice warm wool sweaters. I didn't know!

"The sheep aren't treated nicely when they are being sheared. They are outright abused, from what Enzo told me. Anyway, once they get old, they are sent away to be ..."

Tears stream down my cheeks. I don't wipe them away. Why is this going on? Why is no one doing anything about it?

Miss Honey hands me a tissue. I blow my nose, nodding to show my appreciation. I stop and stare at her. Where did she get a tissue?

"Did you know that Meryl did more in her lifetime than most humans do in theirs? She not only has saved more animals from a factory farm fate but she has made people aware of the inhumane treatment of farmed animals. Laws have been changed because of Meryl and Farmer Harry."

You go girl! And Farmer Harry, too!

"We're not done yet! We have a long way to go. It's a start. A huge step of knowledge of helping animals has been taken in the right direction."

THE DAIRY QUEEN'S DAUGHTER

I look around, notice the morning is awakening, stretching, and welcoming new light on the day — that I'm still not sure I'm having. Even though I'm unsure whether this is a dream or not, I again decide that I have to go with the flow. Why not — I'm safe, I'm learning, and I'm having a good time — in some weird way.

"Each and every animal here at 'The Grave' was special. They were all dear and caring individuals. Mia is buried over here, under this maple tree," she points over her shoulder with her wing. "They called her 'Mama Mia' because of all the babies she took in as a foster mom. Oh, how we all cherished her; she was the matriarch of Animal Haven. She had a good life here, but her life started sad..." Miss Honey shakes her head and looks at me solemnly, "real sad."

"Farmer Harry found Mama Mia when she was only a few days old. Her mama, I guess you could call her 'Grand-mamma Mia,' was a dairy cow. Mama

Mia called her a 'Dairy Queen.' She liked talking all fancy sometimes," Miss Honey says with a smile.

"Did you know that dairy cows must have lots and lots of babies? That's the only way to keep their milk coming and, how can I say this, there's no lovin' going on in the pastures, ya know what I mean? The dairy cows are artificially inseminated every year!"

Miss Honey blushes giving me a strange look as she waits for me to understand what she had just said. It takes me a moment and then I realize, no way! That's awful! That's just ... awful and sick! Those cows look so happy on the milk containers — yes, happy!

"Their daughters, the female calves, are 'saved' because they can produce more milk when they're older. The boys are doomed at birth, just because, they're boys. They become veal. I'll tell you more about them later. Yeah, the dairy farmers snatch their babies away from their mamas soon after they're born. This, I think is also strange and really sad because calves aren't naturally weaned from their moms until after their first birthdays. The dairy ladies have to get right back to work after childbirth. Farmer Harry says that cows cry themselves hoarse when their babies are taken away and they never see them again. Who wouldn't? I'm not a mama," Miss Honey shakes her head sadly, "but my heart breaks for them!"

Cows miss their babies? I never thought of that! And the reason is: for us to have milk, ice cream, and yogurt. But, don't we *need* the calcium from dairy to have strong bones? But ... at the expense of baby calves?

I put my head down as I imagine my cousins as babies being taken away from my aunt. Then I hear a cackling sound. I look up and see Miss Honey is crying. We both seem to pause for a second, then we fall into each other's arms (and wings) crying and trying to console each other with back patting and wing flapping. We stop and just sit there in our own thoughts for a moment or two. Miss Honey then continues as if our shared emotional moment never happened.

"Clearly, these fine ladies, the dairy cows, are pushed to their biological limit," she says clearing her throat. "Such utterly hard jobs these fine mamas have, and there is nothing hoity-toity about any of them either! Good, honest women they are! The cows that live on natural farms, like Animal Haven, can live well past their twentieth birthday. Factory cows become so overweight they can barely walk past their fourth birthday. Sadly, they are then sent off to 'retire.' Some of them think that they are going on vacation. They had a hard life and fantasize they're going to live on some tropical island holding one of those fancy drinks with a tiny umbrella in their hooves. But no, they are hauled off to the slaughterhouse, made into 'cheap meat' hamburgers. These fine hardworking, dignified, overweight, women become fast-food!

"The demands and stress of making and losing their babies *on top* of the conditions of making milk fill them with disease and fatigue. That's right, there is disease and pus in their milk!

Ewww! What?

"Cows are given high-energy food and growth hormones to produce more milk than they would naturally make — about ten times more! All this is so you human folk can have dairy products. Ironic," she cackles, "since 75% of you human folk are even lactose intolerant. That's the sugar part of the milk."

This is so true! I can think of at least five people —no, more! —who actually get sick from dairy. Personally, I know that I can't have feta or blue cheese without becoming very sick for hours. So, why is it then we are told that we need milk to grow and to have strong bones? Why did the hospital push bottle-feeding instead of breast-feeding when my aunt had her babies? Thankfully, she didn't listen. However, what about all the babies who *are* bottle-fed dairy-based formula? Many of my friends' newborn, bottle-fed cousins, and my own nieces and nephews suffered from constipation and diarrhea, colic…and all those ear infections! Could that have been caused from the dairy?!

"And that's not all!" Miss Honey flaps her wings and seems excited to tell me this added bit of news. "New research shows that dairy—especially casein, which is the protein in the milk— is linked with causing cancer in people!"

Cancer! What? I don't understand! From milk?

"What I don't get is that you human folk insist you need your dairy for calcium, right? Enzo, I might have mentioned him before—he's our 'go-to' pig around here. If you have a problem, he's your guy! Anyway, Enzo says that protein in cow's milk is too acidic for your human bodies, and because your body isn't happy with this acidic substance, it fights it by trying to neutralize it. I'm not the type to niggle, but do you know what your body uses to fight it? Come on, guess!" she holds her wings out wide, as if she's challenging me to answer.

I shake my head "no" and put my palms up in the air. I have nothing to say — even if I could speak.

57

"I tell ya, this had us animals so confused about how you human folk reason. Is common sense uncommon with you people?" she asks with a wink. "Did you know that your body uses the calcium that's already *in* your bones to neutralize the milk that you are drinking — sucks it right out it does! That's why lots of your old human folk have bad bones. I tell ya, we weren't just confused, and I don't mean to titter, but we thought it was downright funny how stupid this all is!"

Wait ... what? That makes no sense at all! Let me get this straight: you drink your milk— okay the cow's milk— for calcium to make strong bones, which then makes your body deplete the calcium that's already *in* your bones because cow's milk is too acidic for people in the first place? Hmm, maybe that is that why so many old people have osteoporosis and frail bones. I wonder what would happen if you didn't drink any? I don't understand! My head is throbbing and I'm fuming as I rub my temples.

Silence.

I look at Miss Honey and realize that she knows I'm mad by the expression on my face. Is that a tiny smile I see on her beak? Oh my, is she feeling sorry for me?

"The only purpose for cow's milk is for their tiny baby calf to grow really big — like 800 pounds in a short while, period. All baby animals eventually stop drinking milk, but you human folk are never weaned off. Maybe it *is* best that you folks aren't breast-fed too long." She stops and laughs as she covers her mouth with her wing, "Human kids wouldn't be coming home from college *just* for money. Hehe-haha! And, no wonder most of you human folk are starting to waddle like cows!"

What! Now wait a minute. Just because I can't speak doesn't mean you have to be so insulting. I make a mock-mad face at her, and she smiles. Is she teasing me to make me feel better? Awww!

I get a little rush of excitement. We're bonding. I'm bonding with a turkey? Yeah, I am – and I'm happy about it!

"Can I ask you a question? Why did you guys pick a cow for your main source of dairy? It's breast milk from an *animal* — do you realize that?" she asks as she moves in, beak to nose to me. "Don't you know that certain vegetables have all the calcium you need? And, why not try the milk from different animals for a change? Give those girls a break. Have you ever tried milk from a chimp or a zebra? Why a cow? Just wondering, that's all."

59

I stick out my tongue and then shrug my shoulders. She does have a point though! But, monkey milk and cookies — I don't think so!

"Casein, cancer, 75%, colic…," I quickly write in my notebook before I forget. I stop for a second. Did she say Enzo was a go-to "pig?" Nah, he sounds too smart. He's probably Farmer Harry's farmhand.

"Now where was I? Mama Mia…" Miss Honey perches up a little straighter before she continues. "It was back in the late eighties in a rural stockyard when Farmer Harry saw this tiny black and white cow. Pretty, little girl she must have been. She was sweet, but she was so afraid. She was just lying there, she couldn't walk. She's what they label a 'downed cow.' I mentioned downed animals earlier.

"Downed cows are cows that are too sick to move, real close to death. Some of them are either dragged to the slaughterhouse to be put out of their pain or are left to die wherever they happen to fall. These sick cows are also made into what you call 'fast food hamburgers.'"

Again with the fast-food; these are the meals that most Americans thrive on! This is just so wrong! Why is she telling me this? Then I remember what I wanted: to 'be their voice.' I wanted to know everything. Just take notes. I have to try to distance myself from what she's saying. I can vomit and cry all I want when I go home.

"There are new laws now to protect animals, stop unnecessary and cruel abuse — so we're told. Humane slaughtering of animals is bad enough, but this abuse has been needless sick torture all these years. But," Miss Honey says shaking her head in confusion, "sometimes I wonder why these slaughterhouse and factory farm owners still get mighty mad when people sneak in with those hidden cameras. What are they hiding that they don't want to share with the public human folk?

"AND...!" She says as her back feathers ruffle up. "Sit and make sure you write this down, Reporter.

I sit down and start a brand-new page.

"The law that really confuses me is called 'Ag-gag-laws.' Have you heard of them? These Ag-gag laws are nincompoopy rules to punish the whistle-blowing human folk, such as the investigators and the journalists who sneak in to prove that there is still animal cruelty going on behind those closed doors. Investigators from groups such as *The Humane Society, Mercy for Animals,* and *Compassion Over Killing,* have taken pictures and videos and written about not only frightening animal cruelty but also about human folk health dangers in the food industry.

These hunky-dory, compassionate people are only making sure that the slaughterhouses and factory farms are following the law, but *they* are punished for checking up on them. Makes ya wonder if some skullduggery is happening between the animal agriculture folk and those lawmakers, eh? Why does the government spend more time keeping animal abuse a secret rather than doing something to stop it? Does the government want the American people to stay in the dark about such things?" Miss Honey looks at me.

I don't know. I DON'T know!

Miss Honey struts around, mumbling and gobbling to herself. She shakes her head vibrating her wattle and then lets out a deep sigh, sitting down next to me.

"Back to my story, where were we?" Miss Honey asks, still trying to relax. "Mama Mia? Oh, yea, she couldn't walk. She had an infection in her leg joint and needed surgery. Oh, how the room would come alive at this part of the story. Mama Mia would try and get everyone involved in the excitement of her mood," Miss Honey grins.

"'Now, who's going to take a sick calf to the vet?' Mama Mia would ask in a loud voice to charge up the group who was listening to her story. 'Who's going to take a *little cheap beef patty* like I was and spend big bucks to make them feel better? She'd look around the room for answers and everyone would scream with just as much excitement in their voices as she had in hers."

FARMER HARRY! I mouth as Miss Honey screeches...

"'FARMER HARRY, that's who!'

"He took her to that vet. It cost plenty money, it did, but his heart is so big, it just didn't matter.

"Cows, all animals, are just like people. If you take the chance to get to know them a bit, you'd really like them.

"Mama Mia and Farmer Harry became fast friends. There weren't too many animals at Animal Haven back then, so he had lots of time for her. They got along real fine. They played together, ate together, and Mama Mia learned to trust people again. She was a forgiving girl, but she never forgot.

"Come on over here," Miss Honey points to the path, "I have more friends and more stories for you."

"FOUR GOOD BOYS"

"It was a steamy summer day at the farm," Miss Honey seems to begin her new tale with renewed enthusiasm. "Farmer Harry received an emergency call from the Humane Society soon after Mama Mia was all settled in. They needed to find a safe home for four good boys — calves they were.

"It turned out that two police officers pulled over an old beat-up Dodge because it didn't have any license plates. BOOM, BOOM, BANG, BOOM!" Miss Honey dramatizes by hopping after each word for emphasis. "They heard these sounds coming from the trunk as they were questioning the elderly man. They knew something *bizarre-eerie* was going on in there! You couldn't believe how shocked those two officers were when they opened the trunk and found four, two-day old Jersey calves hog-tied with their front and back legs roped together, and covered in their own poop!"

I'm shaking my head, and my eyes are filling up again. I'm furious! I shake my fist just to show her how mad I am. Why is it against the law that you can't hog-tie this dirty rotten, old man?

"…it was over 100 degrees that day and of course even hotter in that trunk. The police called the Humane Society to come help those poor babies. The vet said they were severely dehydrated and near death. He cooled those babies down with rubbing alcohol, gave them fluids and cow colostrums — that's a calf's first nutrient-rich and immunity-boosting milk," Miss Honey nods, "in an IV, to boost their weak immune systems. He said they reminded him of fawns with those sweet doe like eyes and soft brown skin."

Awww!

"The next few days were touch and go for those babies. They were just so fragile. After a week or two, their condition stabilized. That's when Farmer Harry got that call. He had the perfect mama for those boys, and he was excited to see how Mama Mia would care for them. He was thinking that she needed some babies of her own because of the way she loved the lambs and young goats that were on the farm already.

"These were Mama Mia's first babies. When Farmer Harry brought them home, they acted like curious human folk toddlers: looking all around and touching everything. They mooed at the other cows and were thrilled, giggling with delight, when those cows mooed back at them.

"Then they met their new Mama. I tell ya, it brings tears to my eyes just remembering the look on her face when she met them," she says wiping her eyes with her wings. "Like Christmas morning – no, better – like falling in love! That's what it was — love at first sight for Mama Mia and her new sons."

Note to self: bring tissues the next time you fall and hit your head in the event a turkey tells you emotional stories.

"Sure, they had some problems when they got here," she nods matter-of-factly with a slight wave of her wing. "They were still troubled from their trunk ordeal, who wouldn't be? They'd wake up screaming from nightmares about their young and tragic lives. Mama Mia had all the love and the patience for those boys, so sweet!

"At first they wouldn't eat, and needed to be bottle-fed. They sure enjoyed eating their grains, grass and alfalfa after they were weaned off the bottle. Mama Mia would take them for long walks every day up on the grassy hills to strengthen their little legs. They'd cuddle and nap with her in the afternoon under that big ol' tree." Miss Honey stretches to point at a big tree behind us. "Mama Mia gave them all the love she had in her heart, telling them stories to make them feel good about themselves again and to walk with their heads up high. Like magic, those boys changed into fine young men, or bulls they're called.

"Farmer Harry was getting busier now with new animals. He didn't spend all his time with Mama Mia anymore. She had her own family now, just her and the boys. She was a fine young mama.

"And that beat-up-old Mr. Dodge man, he got just four days in jail — one day for each of the calves that he brutally hog-tied and stuffed in his trunk. Such a snollygoster...!"

A snollygoster? I'd call him a stinkin', rotten, stupid...evil man!

"...I'm not a judge, and I don't know the law, but that just doesn't seem fair to me." Miss Honey shakes her head, looking confused. "What I don't understand is that Mr. Dodge man never said he was sorry. He didn't know — and still doesn't know — that he did anything wrong! If I were a judge, I'd make Dodge-man stay with us for a while at Animal Haven. I would make him work a bit so he'd get to know us. He'd be real sorry then, don't ya think?"

I nod my head up and down exaggeratedly. I want Miss Honey to know that I agree with her.

"One day, Mama Mia woke up and saw Farmer Harry taking her four boys. She didn't know that he had found them good homes where they could live long and happy lives grazing in the hills of a caring family. At first, she didn't think anything of it, but they mooed for her and he just kept takin' 'em. He never told Mama Mia, he just stole them away from her. He carried those boys while they cried for their mama. Mama Mia couldn't understand what was happening. She then remembered being taken away from her mama. She was afraid for her boys — and real sad too. Her heart of gold was shattered. Mama Mia rolled on her back and she cried for days. What a pitiful sound bellowed through the pastures of pleasure. No one could ease her out of her misery. Many tried, but Mama Mia lived a sad life after that day. It was even heartbreaking to see how miserable she lived. She ate just enough to survive, but that was even questionable. She became a shell of the beautiful cow she once was. Farmer Harry didn't know what to do. He had work to do, along with getting new animals, and was away on business for a few weeks after that. Farmer Harry was getting real busy with changing the animal laws.

"The day he came back for a visit, he called for Mama Mia. He missed her a lot. She was his good friend. He was thrilled when he first saw her running to him; he assumed she was better. But when Mama Mia saw Farmer Harry, and heard that man's voice, she wanted to get him. Get him and hurt him! She hated Farmer Harry now 'cuz he was the one who took away her baby boys. He broke her heart *and* her trust. She jogged to him, screaming, 'YOUUUUUUU!' Thank goodness, sense overtook Farmer Harry, and he ran for his life. That big smile on his face changed to fear as he leaped over a fence and landed in the pigs' mud pond before Mama Mia could hurt him. Oh, how silly he looked," Miss Honey covers her beak, stifling a giggle. "We all tried not to laugh, but we just couldn't help ourselves! Not Mama Mia, she just turned and walked away with her head down near to the ground. She probably realized that she had just sunk to a new low.

"Now, don't get me wrong. I'm not saying Farmer Harry was a flibbertigibbet or anything. Mama Mia would later tell this story and make it clear that everyone understood that Farmer Harry was nothing but a calf himself in those days — 'a babe, still wet behind his ears, that man was,' she'd explain, 'he still had lots a' learnin' to do.'"

Yes, yes, yes — I know what you mean!

"Mama Mia forgave Farmer Harry and they became friends again once he explained that her baby boys were happy. Oh, he loved Mama Mia. He never wanted to make her sad, but he just plain didn't know that cows could love and get their feelings hurt, like Mama Mia did, when he took her babies away. He had no idea that animals had emotions — just like people."

Come on, there has to be more to this story. Make it end happily!

THAT'S A LOT OF BULL

"Georgie came to live here at Animal Haven later that year," Miss Honey says. "It was in late fall, I believe. He was born on a dairy farm and snatched away from his mama on the day of his birth, because he was a male calf.

"You ever eat veal parmesan or veal cutlets, Reporter?" Miss Honey questions me while closely looking right into my eyes. She whispers, "That's what he could have been made into. Newborn male calves who are taken away from their mamas and killed right away are cheaper veal — that's called 'bob,' used for pet food. The more expensive or the 'gourmet' veal is from older baby boys. These babies are restrained by the neck, chained, and kept in tiny, inhumane cages that are 30 inches wide by 72 inches long," she says as she holds out her wings to show me the size. "They can't move and make their muscles strong. That's why their flesh is so tender," Miss Honey grimaces, "… and *appetizing* to you human folk. They're taken away from their moms so people can have their milk, and then the calves are fed substitute milk. Isn't that a cockamamie thing to

71

do? Well, this 'food' purposely keeps their iron low so their flesh stays whiter. Don't forget, these are *babies* we're talkin' about! They live out their short lives until, you know, they're slaughtered. So, in other words, veal is a direct result, the flip side of the dairy business, 'cause if you human folk didn't *require* all that milk the babies cows wouldn't have needed to be born in the first place."

Suddenly, I'm having a disturbing flashback. I'm about thirteen years old at my grandparents' house and I'm eating a whitish meat with mushroom gravy. I never thought of "meat" back then. Meat was meat was meat. The meal was good but I later found out that it was veal. I might have asked, or maybe I realized what it was on my own. I didn't want to think about it then, so I didn't - but I never ate it again.

I start retching. My meat could have had a name? A mother? Miss Honey gives me a hard flap on my back with her wing and asks.

"Reporter. Reporter? Are you ok?"

I nod my head "yes," but I think I threw up a little.

"Luck was on Georgie's side that day. The veal farm truck came along once a week to this particular dairy farm, and Georgie just missed his ride. Georgie was such a newborn. He was still wet with afterbirth and was too young to be on his own. He lay on the floor during that freezing cold night, crying and hoping his mama could hear him, help him. He fell asleep. He felt like he was drifting away to a sure death when, thank goodness, Farmer Harry found him. He saw Georgie crumpled up in the corner of the barn. He was dehydrated, his eyes were all sunken in, and he wasn't moving, like a pile of discarded rubbish.

"Farmer Harry asked a stockyard worker what he planned on doing with the calf that was lying down in the corner. Farmer Harry would have gotten into big trouble if he just took him 'cause the newborn was someone else's 'property.' The stockyard worker shrugged his shoulders and said, 'Reckon I'm going to have ta work overtime today and throw out that downer. You can take 'em if you want 'em, it's only garbage.'

"Rage overtook Farmer Harry. He scooped up Georgie and drove him to the nearest vet. The vet took one look at that baby boy and said, 'That calf has only a small chance of survival. Why are you wasting your time and your money? It just doesn't make any dollar sense. *It*'s not worth it.'

"Farmer Harry was blue in the face and raving mad, he yelled, 'That animal needs *our* help and *we* are going to help him! You got that?! And he's NOT an 'it!'" Miss Honey shrieks a little madly, flapping her wings.

You tell him, Farmer Harry! I think I'm starting to feel the beginning of a crush on him. I can't wait to meet him! I wonder if he's cute.

"That poor baby was so hypothermic that his temperature was ten degrees below normal. It was so low that it wouldn't even read on the vet's thermometer. The vet told Farmer Harry that he was going to need colostrum, but he didn't have any. Farmer Harry ran out, banging on all of the dairy farmers' doors until he found a farmer that would give him some of this special milk.

"When they got home, Farmer Harry had to help Georgie develop a suckling reflex, which all the calves learn naturally from their mamas. He had to dip some milk onto his finger and put it into Georgie's mouth. Without a suckling reflex, Farmer Harry was worried that that poor boy would have no will to live.

"Georgie could feel the concern from Farmer Harry. I'm sure Farmer Harry's love probably warmed his little heart!" Miss Honey smiles with a tender look on her face. "We all cheered when Georgie drank his first bottle of milk on his own. What a joyful day it was here at Animal Haven!

"Farmer Harry spent lots of time with Georgie, who was still on an IV and in fragile condition. Georgie was recovering physically, but he wasn't thriving. There was still something missing in that little calf's life. That was when Farmer Harry introduced Georgie to his new mama.

"Mama Mia walked in slowly after being out all day. That lonely, sad heifer spent all of her time by herself. She was even starting to have that unemotional stare in her eyes. She took one look at her new son and heard him cry, 'MAAAAAAA.' You could see it in her eyes that her whole world became more colorful and bright again that instant," Miss Honey grins proudly. "It seemed like there were only two animals in the barn that day — Mama Mia and her new son, Georgie. She ran over to him and loved him like no one could ever dream possible."

More tears, they're happy tears, though. I DO have to stop this!

"Mama Mia had plenty more foster calves during her life due to her never-ending natural maternal instinct, but Georgie, the boy who came into her life when she needed him the most, was her favorite.

"She was a proud mama of Georgie and all of his accomplishments. Georgie was always busy

75

meeting visitors and traveling as an animal activist but he always had time for his mama. All of her children loved her even when they were all grown up. They'd visit her, bring her flowers and alfalfa, sit with her in the sun, and make her laugh. That's how you see all the good you've done in your life —through the eyes and in the actions of the ones you love.

"Mama Mia, who gave so much love during her life, ironically died on Valentine's Day. She slowed down the last few months, not eating much. We all knew, and I think she did too, that her time with us was almost done. It gave us all a chance to say good-bye," Miss Honey whispers, struggling with the words. She was a real beauty, Mama Mia, even in her old age. She had a certain grace and a magic about her that lasted her whole long and happy life.

"Now, Georgie, he grew up to be real big — massive, you could say — and strong, strong like a really big bull. Male cows that are not castrated are referred to as bulls, whereas the boys who have been castrated are called steers. As I said, his birth mom was a dairy cow and she was given artificial growth hormones to make her muscles develop faster than normal. He grew to be 3,000 pounds and six feet tall. And that Georgie had a big personality to match his massive size. He was no namby-pamby bull! Visitors were actually afraid of him when they first saw him, but he was such a gentle giant, a warm cow, and he loved affection. A real people person, I mean, a people bull, ya know?

"People adored him when they got to know him. He just had a charismatic way about him. Took after his mom, he did! He'd joke with the visitors and say, 'I could have been your parents' prime rib dinner on the day they married.' Mama Mia didn't like him joking like that and would scold him, 'Hush boy, don't you have disrespect for who you are.' But he loved teasing her. He'd apologize for *beefing* her up, he'd say to her with a wink, and she'd just roll her eyes in mock sarcasm and mosey away. They had a playful relationship like that. He spoke this way because he wanted people to make the connection that *their meat* once had a name, a personality, and real feelings.

"Georgie didn't have a formal education, as Romeo had, but he did have that certain natural kind of instinct for what to say. It was a gift. He had the visitors thinking when they heard about his life, and they'd fall in love with him. Plenty of our visitors became vegetarians. I think Georgie knew what he was doing," she adds with a smile.

"This all started when Georgie was just a boy. He felt it in his heart that he *could* make a difference. Maybe it was even, what you might say a 'calling' — or a '*mooing*' in his case." She looks at me for a reaction. "He wanted to become an advocate for his friends."

I love Georgie! What a good boy! I'm having a hard time thinking of him as a bull. I can't wait to meet him too!

"He and Mama Mia talked about his vocational instinct one day in the pastures of pleasure. 'Ma, when I grow up, I wanna help other animals just like Farmer Harry helped us. I can do it Ma, I know I can!'

"Mama Mia didn't want her boy to leave her, but she knew she had to do the right thing. She had to share her son with Farmer Harry, and the world.

"'Georgie, you go and have a talk with Farmer Harry today. You are a good, special young man with a lot of *oomph* in you. People will listen to you and your story. They'll change the laws because of you. Now you pay attention to your mama and you go, now!'"

"Georgie became the Ambassador of Animal Haven that year. That was also the year that his voice changed into a man's voice — a bull's moo," Miss Honey says smiling. "Georgie wasn't a calf

78

anymore. His deep mooing voice commanded
respect and attention. Farmer Harry was working on
a special campaign when he and Georgie traveled to
Washington, DC. Georgie understood Farmer Harry's
work was going to help him, his friends, and all future
animals.

"They both were exhausted after a few days of
speech making, leafleting, picketing, and
campaigning for humane people to get elected into
office, and they decided to take the afternoon off.
They found a nice shady spot to relax under a tree
overlooking the Lincoln Memorial. They needed a
break. They deserved it!"

Miss Honey pauses for a moment and turns her
head trying to compose herself. She looks at me,
wipes her eyes again with her wing, and scrunches
up her face before continuing.

"I am sorry but I do tend to get emotional, ya
know? Okay, so where was I? Georgie and Farmer
Harry wanted people to know that factory farming is
the number one cause for global warming,
deforestation, species extinction, and pollution in the
world," said Miss Honey looking me in the eyes and
explaining in a serious voice. "They wanted them to
know how full of malarkey many people are because
they don't realize that the main cause of death is

from a poor diet, which mainly includes eating animals. These are facts I'm tellin' ya – not pipe dreams."

What! Pollution? My hand hurts from all the notes I'm taking.

"Georgie must have dozed off while reflecting on his week and making plans for the next day. He dreamt of a world of people making choices - smart and compassionate choices about what they ate. He dreamt of a greener world, one with more vegetables and plants. He dreamt how these empathic people would finally put a stop to all those poor animals suffering and dying so inhumanely. 'WHY!' he shouted as he woke up startling Farmer Harry. Georgie looked at him and said, 'I just had a dream!'

"An important law was passed that year, thanks to Farmer Harry and Georgie. The law prevents the marketing and slaughtering the 'downers' or cows too weak or sick to walk with dignity to their deaths in the slaughterhouse."

Wow, good for them! What a wonderful accomplishment, but it's sad that something so sick had to be stopped with a law and not just common sense.

"I know it doesn't sound like much, but it was another small step in the right direction. And like

Romeo says, 'Ignorance is bliss, but when you have knowledge, you then have a responsibility!' Many more people are becoming responsible, but there's still not enough — yet.

"Georgie lived a long, happy, and productive life, but due to his huge size, he developed legs-and-joints disease. He lived with the other cows who suffered the same condition in the special needs cow barn here at Animal Haven."

Huh? Did she say, 'lived'? Georgie's...?

"They spent their days lying in the pastures in the sunshine, telling stories about the past, reminiscing only about the good times, and discussing the new animals and all the new laws that might be passed in the near future.

"Georgie was in agony. He needed supplements and pain medicine as well as joint injections. He developed pneumonia. We then found out Georgie also had cancer.

"We all held a vigil by his side the last night. He was still the same ol' Georgie, joking and trying to make us all feel better. He still ate his carrots with the enthusiasm of a young, healthy calf.

Oh no...! I cover my mouth. No...! I bat away the tears that are building up. Georgie, he's...?

"Georgie left us that night. It was quick and peaceful. Georgie died with dignity and the love of his friends around him." Miss Honey pauses for a moment waiting for me to compose myself. "He died knowing his life mattered and changed people's feelings. Heartache like this isn't easy to accept and to live with, but that big ol' Georgie will always be alive in our hearts." She reaches over and rests her wing on my arm. "Now here I'm telling *you* the story about him and he will now live on in your heart forever, too. That's special — *real* special!" She nods enthusiastically while giving me a sympathetic smile. "He no longer belongs to us at the farm. I'm not sure he ever did." Miss Honey looks up, and with a raised wing she says, "He belongs now to the ages."

I shake my head sadly as I try to come to terms with it, Georgie's dead?! I was really hoping to chat with this magnificent, caring cow. I close my eyes as the tears well up. Defeated, I just let them cascade down my face. Miss Honey walks away, somehow sensing that I need to be alone for a moment to mourn a friend that I could have had, but sadly will never even meet.

ROMEO, OH ROMEO!

"Earlier than the first rooster crows! Well, I am certainly glad you came here early Reporter," Miss Honey chirps happily. "That's good. I like that. Let's take a walk to the henhouse, and I'll tell you about some of the birds. We can't sit here all day telling stories, ya know. Are you ready?" Miss Honey asks as she extends a wing to help me.

I compose myself; gather my things again; stretch my arms and legs; and give them a little shake. I twist my head, working out the kinks, while trying to take it all in — where I am and what I'm doing. Then I glance at Miss Honey and notice that she's staring at me.

Miss Honey inhales deeply while looking around surveying the day, "Smell that, Reporter? That's early morning fresh dew. It's a good, clean smell, isn't it? This is my favorite time of the day, the hour after dawn. All is peaceful and quiet right before a new beginning starts. It's the time of day I do yoga after my jog. I like to meditate, ya know. I vow to live my life in harmony with all our fellow companions here, animals as well as human folk."

Well, good for her, now isn't she a down-to-earth kind of turkey?

"Follow me. The bird barn is right over the hill. Yep, the best birds in the world live here at Animal Haven!"

I'm still writing notes, but I can listen and write at the same time. Let's see: *Georgie will always be alive in our hearts...He belongs now to the ages*, got it! I take a deep breath to clear my mind and then follow Miss Honey. We walk only a few feet, and Miss Honey stops and turns to me.

"Romeo, he's the *Pecker* of the House here at Animal Haven, and he *really* lives up to his name, I tell ya! You can interview him when I leave for a while. He will be more than happy to take over your tour. I have to get my ingredients for the mashed clover I'm making for the Thanks-Living feast.

"Romeo, he has an interesting story about his life before coming to the farm, that's where he was educated. Sometimes he uses those fancy big words, and I get all confused. He does seem to *misunderestimate* me at times. He'll then say it a little simpler, but in a nice way of course. I tell him, 'Romeo, Romeo, please don't talk *down* to me.' He'll laugh and laugh because he knows I don't mean duck or goose down. Please, I would never say

something so insulting and hurtful," Miss Honey
shakes her head. "Do you know our feathered friends
have to be ... *harmed* in order for their feathers to be
collected to make those down blankets and all?"

No, I didn't know that! Umm, I suppose that I
thought that someone followed the ducks around all
day and collected their feathers as they naturally fell
off the birds, or maybe scooped them up off the barn
floor at the end of the day. What would be so wrong
with that? But, harmed?!

"Romeo gets me, ya know? He *really* truly
understands me. He's such a scallywag —he is! If
only I were a chicken! But he's got his wives."

Wives? Huh?

"Romeo was born at an elementary school in
an incubator. He's a very intelligent man, like I said,
and boy can he charm the ladies!

"A little known fact about chickens is that
they're smart — smarter than ya think. Do you know
what will happen if one accidentally sees you
opening and unlocking a gate? All the chickens will
be dancing around the farm the next day, running
right at you for fun. You heard the term 'playing
chicken'? That's where they got it, I think.

"Another fact is that a rooster has many wives,
just like Romeo. Some roosters have up to 20 wives.

85

Hehe haha! It's okay, don't look so shocked, the wives know each other! They're good friends; raise their chicks together as a big happy family."

Well, okay then, I don't know the rules of the chicken coops, so I'm not going to judge.

"Sure, sometimes the hens will have their squabbles, but they work it out. The hens, they love their babies. They're a little overprotective, if you ask me," Miss Honey holds up her wing defensively. "But like I said, I'm not a chicken and it's really none of my business.

"If any of the chicks are ever in danger from people, the hens have been known to land on them, spur, and peck them. Hey, that's just who they are and what they do, but I tell ya, you don't wanna mess with their chicks!

"Did you know that hens love to build nests? Romeo's ladies are always competing with each other trying to gussy them up with fancy ribbons and flowers and such. I think they even have the 'prettiest nest contests.' It's all in good fun," Miss Honey nods smiling, taking only a few more steps as she speaks.

"Obviously, the hens also like their privacy when they're laying eggs! Really, who wouldn't? At night, they protect their babies by sitting on them.

Those cute little faces peak out from under their mother's behinds — precious babies, those chicks!

"Sometimes, those babies are as big as their mamas, they are! Romeo once had a good talking with one of his ladies about babying their chicks too long. He's only the rooster, what does he know? The hens rule the roost at Animal Haven, and that's okay. Romeo is outnumbered here, but there's lots of love at the henhouse — lots!

"The chickens are sociable and curious about people. They think you people are real strange lookin', bein' you guys don't have beaks and feathers.

"Romeo's hens, they worship him! Every morning, after he serenades them, his ladies crowd around him, adoringly grooming his feathers while pecking kisses on his face. Romeo, he treats his ladies right. He makes certain they all eat first when the food is delivered, and he takes what's left over. He's such a gentleman! At night, he doesn't go to bed until he checks on all of his wives, gives them each some individual attention. If there's a low flying hawk darting around, you can hear Romeo shrill from miles away to warn his families! Did you know that chickens have 30 different calls? Happy sounds, sad sounds, romantic sounds. Yup! That's my — I mean our — Romeo. He's such a good, loving friend he is."

I nod with a smile. Maybe it's good I have no voice today. I'm not sure I agree with him having so many wives. Miss Honey might not have liked my comments, but he sounds like an okay guy.

"Now our Romeo, he's humble and won't boast about himself, so allow me to share more about him while we stroll," Miss Honey says with a wing flutter.

Suddenly, Miss Honey begins to walk quickly in short hurried steps. It's an awkward pace for me to keep up with, but I try. She continues to chatter as we make our way up and down hills and duck under low branches.

"We might bump into a few others before we get to the bird barn. Watch your head. Hurry up a little bit please, I don't want to miss him. This way now ... We've already wasted enough time...," she mutters as she gives me a quick impatient glance.

I get a feeling that she's blaming me for something. Did I take too much of her time? What about my tour?

We walk through a few bushes, and Miss Honey flaps her way up a hill as I try to trot next to her. Are we late for a meeting? She stops abruptly and leans against a tall tree smiling. I see a heart with initials carved into it. As I bend down to get a better look, Miss Honey quickly covers it with one wing and gives me a slight nudge away from the tree with the other.

"Good! We didn't miss him. Let's wait over here for a bit, and we can talk," she says as she continues pushing me a few trees away.

"For a while, Romeo worked in the office at Animal Haven before he moved into the bird barn. Those birds took to him right away when he arrived here. He is so sweet natured and all. Everybody loves him!

"Did you know visitors come back to Animal Haven *just* to visit him every year? Good friends he's made over the years! I overheard someone once say that he's got mojo, but between you and me," she whispers covering her beak with the tip of her wing, "I don't think he knows a Moe or a Joe."

"Like I said earlier, he's always had a way with the women, even back in the day when he worked with the older, special needs ladies for a while. He was very gentlemanly and showed them great respect—they adored that. He'd open the barn door, and he'd treat them like queens. And what a good dancer he is! I remember one old hen who adored him years ago. What was her name? Linda? Diane?

Yeah, I think it was Diane. Anyway, he's got it all going on for him! Those old hens would fall off their perches when he sang to them.

"Did you know that he even made a record? He sings mostly Sinatra, Louis Armstrong, and Perry Como…oh, and he idolizes Dean Martin. The old crooners, ya know, typical love songs — very romantic. His face is even on an album cover! My – I mean that – Romeo leaves a trail of fainted foul whenever he sings."

She takes my arm with her wing, and we stroll towards a barn that I can now see in the distance.

"There was some talk back then about him going on tour. He decided what he wanted was to start a few families and stay here at Animal Haven. I'm not even sure how he knows how many wives he has!" She giggles.

How do you say "hubba-hubba" in chicken?

"WHOOOA! Wait a minute. STOP!" Miss Honey shrieks as she comes to a stop, blocking me from taking another step with her wings. "Here come those Easter chicks! *Look* at them — no, don't look at them. I don't know. Ya gotta be real nice to these chicks, they're fragile. Anyway, that's what their shipping box was labeled.

"Good morning ladies! Isn't it a beautiful morning?" Miss Honey says sweetly.

All of a sudden, about two dozen young chickens in an array of bright colors - pink, purple, green, blue - sashay past us. I nod and smile to look friendly. They are cute — in a comical way though. However, it's not their appearance that I find so amusing, but their arrogant manner.

"Wait until they pass us by. Well, whoop-de-doo and la-de-da, they didn't even look at us! They have an attitude problem, they always do, those Easter chicks — highfalutin frippets! I do feel sorry for them though. They walk around with their beaks up so high that I worry about them drowning during a spring rain. That's all we need here — a bunch of colorful fluff lying around," Miss Honey grumbles.

I silently giggle at the thought.

"Every year the Animal Haven receives boxes of these chickens that come in all different colors. This year we have over 50 of them. They must know that they're silly looking, but they walk around like they're all high society or something. It's a degrading and disrespectful thing to do. It trivializes who chickens are. So sad that some people think of them as *items* that can be thrown away when they don't want them after the holiday.

"You see, right before Easter, you human folk like experimenting on chicks. Either food coloring is injected into incubating eggs or it is sprayed onto hatchlings to make them look *cute*. They're supposed to be Easter 'novelties,' but like I said, it messes them up emotionally. They stick together in a clique, but I call it '*a cluck*,'" Miss Honey says, emphasizing the word while sticking out her tongue. "They come here with such low self-esteem. Come on, *LOOK* how pathetic they look," she says as she points at them with her wing.

"We try and make them feel good about themselves with counseling and *peep* talks — to boost their confidence in themselves. Apparently, a little too much, ya know. As you just saw, we end up with a bunch of sorry looking snobs. They'll molt and eventually blend in with the rest of the chickens, but they'll always still have issues."

"Weren't you the one who tried to color me with that
dye?
Oh no, not I,
I will survive oh,
as long as I have my ducks, I know I'll stay alive.
I've got all my life to live,
I've got all my love to give and I'll survive,

I will survive!"

What the...!

"It's Peterson, Mallard, and Meredith practicing for the feast! We call them 'Peter, Mall and Merry.' Don't they sound marvelous?" Miss Honey smiles as she nods steering me *away* from the singing with her wing. "Merry is messing with the Easter chicks. We won't bother the musical trio, they don't *like* to be bothered, anyway. Besides, they kinda scare me," she whispers. "They're a bit persnickety 'cause they're from New York City. They're another Easter *horror* story —'leftovers,' they're called.

"Before Easter, the pet stores get extra holiday animals — now what the *beak* is a 'holiday animal,' right? People think rabbits, ducks, and chickens make good gifts. Give a stuffed doll, why don't ya!" Miss Honey shrieks in annoyance. "They don't think of the care and the responsibility that comes along with having a pet, and then these animals often get abused, neglected, or returned — or thrown out!

"These guys were holiday leftovers at the pet store. Thing-a-ma-jigs. Curwhibbles! Nobody wanted them. I guess that's good *and* bad. Merry, the chick, was placed in with the two ducks, Peter and Mall, at the pet store, and those three made a New York City kinda' bond never to be separated from each other. They like to keep to themselves, but they sure are entertaining! Peter and Mall can honk any song in perfect harmony, and Merry can melt any American rooster's heart!

Miss Honey whispers, "I'm not one to tittle-tattle, but we had some problems here at the henhouse after the concert last month. Romeo wanted to harmonize with Merry, and his wives were upset. Like I said, I don't want to gossip, and everything is okay now. Anyway, they must be practicing for the Thanks-Living feast, which reminds me...I have to get that clover. Let's go and find Romeo. He's probably letting his ladies sleep a little late today. Wait until you meet him. Romeo's beak is as red as the roof of the barn! What a man!"

"IGNORANCE IS NOT BLISS"

"If I had you, could I ever want more corn?
It's just impossible
And tomorrow, shouldya ask me for the farm,
somehow I'd get it
I would sell my very comb
and not regret it

"That's him," Miss Honey sighs. "Just listen…melts your heart, it does. I don't want to disturb him. I want to just listen and savor. Ahhhh…" Miss Honey closes her eyes, swaying from side to side with crossed wings at her heart.

For to live without your love—
It's just impossible…"

He *is* quite good!

"Miss Honey?" Romeo calls in a singsong voice as he struts out of the barn. "Is that you? I was just thinking about you. Now, don't you look as attractive as ever? I say, every time I see you… there is just that certain charm. Did you lose a little weight?"

Miss Honey giggles as she quickly adjusts her glasses and fluffs out her golden breast feathers a little.

"Not that you had to," Romeo quickly corrects himself. "You just look extra pretty today. Is that a new scarf? Oh, oh … have you had your coffee beans today?" He winks. "Now that's a preposterous question. Of course you did. I'm sure! Here're a few more. I've been saving them for you."

"What did I tell you, a real charmer, huh?" Miss Honey whispers to me with a silly grin.

Yes you did, I answer nodding with a smile. He's not bad looking either —for a rooster I mean. He has a classic, old-world look about him. Similar to a cool guy from the 50's. His red comb seems to be slicked straight up — with gel? Umm, the faux leather jacket he's wearing is a nice touch too! No wonder the ladies like him; he comes bearing gifts and compliments: Did you lose a little weight? Ha! All guys are the same!

"Thank you Romeo, aren't you sweet," Miss Honey giggles again as she bats her eyelashes.

Well, would you look at them! Miss Honey is a nervous, silly schoolgirl around him. She likes him!

And, he's just as bad— charmer and a flirt! Huh! Turkeys have eyelashes?

"How *are* you? The chicks…the wives, it's been a while — yesterday? Are you all ready for the feast?"

"I know it's your favorite holiday, Miss Honey, and yes, we are ready. The ladies are still working on the beautiful flower centerpieces and crowns. Now I do not want to go and spoil any surprises but the decorations are going to be nice, real nice. And the chicks, well, they're staying out of the way the best they can even though they sure love to play and get into mischief. Now who is this friend you have with you?" Romeo asks as he takes a step closer to examine me. "Are you new here at Animal Haven? Will you be staying for the feast?"

I shyly nod and smile. I feel a little foolish, since I have no voice. I'm sure Miss Honey will explain.

"This is our visitor. Her name is Reporter. She's lost her voice. It still might be here on the farm," she shakes her head after lifting up a small rock. "We're not sure. Have you seen 'it' by chance with the chickens?" Miss Honey asks while shrugging both her wings. "I found her all befuddled by the entrance early this morning, lying in a ditch. She wants to interview the animals here at Animal Haven and…

97

did you say that you'll be writing a book about us?"
Miss Honey asks me but not waiting for a response,
she continues. "Would you, could you, spare some
time, Romeo, and just tell her your story? I'd really
appreciate it, and if I'm not back in time, would you
both walk to the pigs? I have to get some fresh
ingredients for my mashed clover."

A 'book' — a REAL book? I was just taking
notes for a story! I didn't think it was an official book!

"For you, my dear Miss Honey, I will walk to the
ends of the farm. Where did you say you were going
for your clover?"

This cool rooster has all the right lines. How
many wives does he have again?

"The sweetest clover is growing in the forest,
right past the double tree," Miss Honey explains
while pointing with her wing. "The early morning
clover is always covered with fresh dew. Oh, it's
making my mouth water just talking about it!"

"That's not *over* the fence, is it dear Honey?
You know it's not safe for us to leave the gates of
Animal Haven," warns Romeo shaking his head.
"The morning moon is still out, it's called the
'Hunter's Moon,' and that makes me very uneasy, it
does."

"The clover is as wild as you are my Romeo, and I'm sure it will be well worth the trip." Miss Honey smiles, forgetting that I'm here, and then clears her throat before continuing, "No need to mollycoddle me! I'll be careful, and I won't be long. I know my way. I'll get it and come right back here, to you — to the farm, I mean. I have to go right away. Bye!"

"Be safe, my dear Miss Honey, be safe!"

My new pal is leaving me! I run over to Miss Honey and give her an awkward hug. It's not easy to hug a turkey with the wings and all. I try to say 'thank you' and 'be safe,' but my voice still isn't working, so I just give her a silly wave. The big smile she gives me makes me feel like I just made a good friend happy: warm and fuzzy, or would that be *feathery*?

"So, my friend, a reporter," Romeo speaks, now giving me his full attention. "Please perch yourself, I mean, sit right here. I hope you have a little time because I *do* enjoy talking. Miss Honey mentioned that you lost your voice. Huh! Is that true? Perhaps, you have a new voice. Have you tried gobbling like a turkey? Come on, give it a try."

I shake my head 'no, that I haven't' and I figure why not as I then try my best imitation of a turkey gobble. Why am I doing this? I manage to look foolish. I can see my spit spraying out into the

99

sunshine. Was that a booger that just flew out of my nose, too?

"Okay then, still not working?" Romeo shouts, holding up his wing for me to stop trying.

"I'm sure my dear Miss Honey was the perfect hostess," Romeo says, changing the subject. "Such a dear, sweet gal, that Miss Honey. There is nothing that dear gal won't do. If she were only a chicken..." He looks away for a moment. "I hope she'll be okay. She does take chances at times to help others. So giving — always so very giving she is!"

This rooster does have a serious thing for the Miss Honey! I grin and nod; however, he seems deep in his thoughts and doesn't notice.

"OK, so, *my* story, let me see, it's been a while. My name is Romeo, Romeo Romero." He stretches out his wing for me to shake. "I was the only survivor of an elementary school baby chick hatching project. The students considered me a 'learning tool,' and I hope they learned more than the fact that their teacher lacked proper preparation skills. The teacher had no plan on what to do with me or even how to care for me after I hatched. Don't you people use the term, 'duh' for a situation like this, am I right?" Romeo says with an unblinking stare inches from my face.

100

I nod, again, as if I fully understand him. I gesture, 'Of course,' with my hand.

"…but she did allow…" Romeo says sadly, "my brother and I — rest his soul — to hatch!" He raises a wing to the sky and looks up before he continues. "The *experiment* was to crack an egg open every day so the children could see our growth stages. What is wrong with you people? Don't they have this information on the Internet?

"So, I hatched, the kids cheered and — then what? Thank goodness, one of the moms took me to Animal Haven when I was only a few hours old. I was still wet from the shell and could have caught a wicked cold and died!

"One of the caregivers here became my guardian angel, cared for me twenty four-seven for a few months. She is still a good friend of mine, a dear godmother to some of the chicks, she is. There was nothing she wouldn't do for me. She knitted a tiny papoose to carry me around in, and she even took me home at night. We would watch David Letterman and the old black and white movies. She fed me the best seed. What a dear she was – my savior – really!" Romeo says smiling.

Really! You've watched David Letterman? Get outta here!

"When I got a little bit stronger I worked in the office for a while, nothing important, just some light filing and simple computer work. I enjoyed learning by listening to human folk. That is how I became informed about the fate of most factory animals. When I first heard these conversations, I thought that they were talking about some science fiction movie, didn't think much of it. Then one day I realized that it was *real* life. Let me tell you, I was so frightened that I crawled in my papoose and wouldn't come out for days! I would wake up screeching from my dreams. It took a long time for them to convince me that I was safe here and nothing bad would ever happen to me. My people folk at the office would comfort me when they saw me crying." Romeo pauses with a smile as he reminisces. "Truth be told, I enjoyed being cuddled on everyone's laps. Oh, I loved that! That could be the reason why I'm still such an affectionate rooster. As a young chick, I guess I needed some extra tender loving care and mothering — being an orphan and all. I decided that I would find a way to help. I didn't know exactly what I'd do, but I knew that a good education was the answer to solve many of the farm's problems.

"Enzo was saying that a friend of his — I think they were friends — Nelson Mandela, once said that,

'Education is the most powerful weapon which you can use to change the world.'

Enzo... Miss Honey talked about him. Who was he again? She mentioned his name before — the farmhand? Wow, he knew Nelson Mandella?!

"Anyway, I truly believe that there's a reason for everything. I believe I just wasn't hatched to be a regular rooster. Maybe my mission in life is to inform people folk somehow. My mantra is, 'Ignorance is bliss, but when you have knowledge, you then have a responsibility.' So with my knowledge, I try my best to educate others, but you know what?" Romeo shakes his head sadly, "Ignorance is not bliss — for us! Ignorance is indifference, it's violence, it's inhumane, uncaring ... ignorance is an excuse to look the other way — but ignorance is what it is!" Romeo shrugs hopelessly, appearing tired and defeated. "A rooster can only do so much," he says shaking his head.

"Okay, back to my story. Not long after my office career, Farmer Harry decided it was time for me to move into the chicken coop; apparently he needed a new manager."

He knows Farmer Harry, too? Where is this guy! I start 'goose-necking' to find him. Is 'goose necking' a politically correct phrase on a farm?

"…Farmer Harry didn't want to spoil me, and I've come to understand that after becoming a father. To be honest, I was nervous at first living there. What did I know about chickens, except for being one? I immediately felt at home. I loved being who I am: a chicken! I was finally with my peeps!

"My hobbies are dancing and singing," Romeo adds grinning, "My music has more charms to soothe the savage beast around here — not that we have any — but I've wooed many a fine hen with my musical talents… yep, many a fine hen."

Modest, isn't he?

"Also, years ago, I teamed up with a cow, Ray-Gee — a good friend of mine. We had a song and comedy gig at a barnyard club – called ourselves, 'Cock-n-Bull Brothers.' Somewhat of a Beatles fanatic he was." Romeo says with a cackle. "You should have seen those heifers dropping like swatted flies when he sang," He clears his throat and begins, *'something in the way she moos, attracts me like no utter lover.'* he shakes his head laughing. "Those were the days my friend, *those* were the days. And, that's all I have to say about me."

I nod my head 'yes.' I look up from taking notes. Wait, WHAT did he just say? 'Wooed hens?' 'A barnyard club?'

THE PLIGHT OF THE CHICKENS

"One of my greatest thrills is speaking with visitors who come to visit us here at Animal Haven," Romeo boasts proudly with his head held high. "I feel extremely complimented when they return and ask specifically for me.

"I like to consider myself a family man. Am I henpecked? Perhaps, but I do love my wives and my children. I have a good life here.

"But the other chickens, the ones on the outside, have terrible, simply terrible lives. It is inexcusable what they endure, and it's scarier than anything I've ever seen on those late night horror and science fiction movies. I have to share with you," he whispers, indicating for me to lean in, and when I do he quickly looks around to make sure that no one is listening. "I can't risk any of my wives, or heaven forbid, my young chicks hearing this. They do not know, nor do I want them to know! They see the rescued chickens coming here, hear rumors, but I don't discuss these horrors with the wives and the chicks. It's too disturbing."

105

He suddenly stops and sadly looks at me shaking his head. "I suppose my inactions fall into that 'Ignorance is bliss' category too.

"First, the living conditions for those poor chickens are horrendous. Do me a favor, please, and close your eyes."

I look at him suspiciously.

"Come on now, humor me, close them tight." He says with a wing nudge. "Are they closed? No peeking now, okay?" Romeo asks. I can feel his breath on my cheek as he stares at my face closely.

This rooster tells me to close my eyes and I do it. Who is the crazy one here? I nod. My eyes ARE closed! But, I kinda wanna peek.

"Imagine you are in an elevator with twelve other people," he begins to explain, "squished together with no windows or real doors — a lot like an elevator. It's really bigger than this and so many more chickens, and for your fantasy — we'll say 'people' but you get the picture, right?"

I nod.

"This is your home. This is where you live, eat, sleep, and relieve all your bodily functions. The ammonia smell from everyone's urine is so overpowering that your eyes burn and you will probably develop a respiratory infection as well as other diseases. A few of your friends and or family members may have died and remain here — rotting! Your food is scattered on the floor covered in all of this!"

Ewwww! I dry heave, open my eyes, and cover my mouth. Why is he telling me this?

Romeo stares at me and waits until I close my eyes again before continuing.

"Yeah, right, and all this is going on in your 'home sweet home.' You and the others naturally get on each other's nerves and begin pecking at each other. As a result, your beaks, bear with me now, will be removed - without any anesthesia!! That's right, clipped right off!"

I open my eyes nervously and take a few steps back. That's it! I don't want to keep them closed anymore. Romeo's tirade is getting a little heated, and I'm nervous that he might take his anger out at me — while my eyes are closed, no less. I don't think so! Besides, what is he talking about? Who would treat chickens this way?

"One wife, Deb-E, still shudders when she thinks about the pain she felt. She since clucks with a lisp when she's angry. She is still my special gal. I love her!" Romeo says dreamily.

He shakes his head before he continues, "Oh, so you get medicine for your various diseases and growth shots to make you grow larger — larger than what your grandparents were. You feel all alone, even though you are living with hundreds— thousands of other chickens going through the same experience you are. You are treated like a 'thing' instead of like a being who can feel pain and experience emotions. Moreover 'things,' regretfully so, are subjected to cruel treatment— which I will NOT talk about!

"The *lucky* chickens get to live on a 'free range' or a 'cage free' farm. Have you heard these terms before? What a marketing hype that is!" He says a little louder. "That means the tiny door, way across the room, is open a little bit! HELLO! They should be thankful for *that*?" Romeo asks, shrugging up his wing questionably. "And I know for a fact that human folk do not like to be treated badly. You do realize, I have seen all the *Planet of the Ape* movies. Human folk get so misled by these feel-good certified *humane* treatment labels, but these chickens still go to the same slaughterhouse!

Wait a minute, it just dawns on me, is Romeo talking about the chickens that you eat? They treat them like that? That's NOT right! That's just not right for the chickens — or people. They say chicken is much healthier to eat than red meat too – but who are "they?"

I must have eaten, umm… how many chickens in my life? I add up in my notebook: Two chickens a week, let's say; times four weeks in a month, is eight; okay now, eight chickens times twelve months is…; and then multiply that by eighteen. I shake my head in horror and gulp as I quickly hide my calculations from Romeo. My hand is over the number '1,728.' I've eaten almost two thousand chickens my life!

Romeo doesn't notice my nervousness and continues, "And, our sweet egg-laying gals are the most abused of all the farm animals. Enzo was telling me in 2007, that 280 million hens laid 77.3 billion eggs. That is roughly 250 eggs a year each, which is 150 *more* eggs than what they would naturally lay. I was thinking about becoming their union leader years ago, when I was younger, with strikes and posters, but that didn't work out. It was just a thought though." He chuckles, "youth!"

"So, you'd think they would entice these hardworking, egg-laying women to work even harder by sweet-talking them or giving them a little time off. NO, they starve them instead!" Romeo screeches with his eyes bugging out. "Yep, that's right, for up to two weeks the egg companies can get away without feeding them. This methodology, called 'force molting,' shocks their bodies into laying eggs faster.

"And you think the working conditions would be nice, huh? Nope, they are as dirty and disgusting as the other chickens' living arrangements I mentioned before. Ninety-five percent of these egg-laying hens live in battery cages that confine the chickens to about the dimensions of a letter-sized paper each. This practice is so cruel that it's banned in many nations in Europe, but not here. Not in the good USA!"

I get up and walk away.

"Wait, I'm not done yet," Romeo shouts as he follows me. "I know it's hard to believe, but it gets worse! You have to hear this and write this in your book."

I stop and look at him. My book? He's not going to give up but —he is right, so I sit and write what he tells me.

"The chicks that are hatched for future egg laying are separated from their mothers at birth. The females are spared to carry on with the business, but the males are of no use," he hesitates before finishing, "so they are ground up *live* for fertilizer."

LIVE?! My head swings up from my notebook. What?! These are precious balls of living fluff. That's not right. I shake my head in disbelief. That's insane!

"I think of my wives and my chicks when I hear these horror stories. I get so angry that I can't do anything. These are living beings with personalities and feelings. Human folk use the expression 'mother hen' for overprotective moms. Hens are deprived of exercising this natural instinct — and they make great moms too," he flutters his wings in disgust. "Most of these mothers end up losing their minds and stay alive just long enough to be violently slaughtered!" Romeo screeches, as he angrily looks right into my eyes.

I suddenly feel as if he doesn't like me, I know it. Romeo thinks I'm a chicken eater. I'm NOT. I mean, I was in the past but – not anymore. Sure, I've eaten chicken before – but I didn't know. That means I am — NO, I was —one of them. I'll go 'cold turkey,' I can't say that — I mean, I can't think that. I cover my face in shame. I'm sorry. I am so, so sorry. I quickly cross out my number '1,728' but now it looks like a big black – egg! Oh, no! I doodle a flower on top of it.

Romeo sits down on a pile of hay looking exasperated. He fans his blushed cheeks with his wing, and wearily stares at the ground, blinking back tears.

"It gets even worse, but I believe I've said that already. Are you ready for more? I *have to* tell you the rest."

I nod, indicating for him to continue, but I don't know how much more I can take.

"Chickens, all poultry in the United States, are excluded from the Humane Methods of Livestock Slaughter Act. This law is supposed to protect the animals by requiring them to be numb to pain before they are killed. The machines on the assembly at the factory farms *are* just that — machines, and machines do tend to malfunction occasionally, right? They say the chickens are 'bird-brained' and have no feelings. You know, I was hatched, but I was not hatched yesterday, if you know what I mean. This just is not right, but this is the ways of the world - a very sick world.

"I'm sorry. I cannot go on. I'm too upset. I cannot even think about it anymore. I would not wish this treatment on my worst enemy. NO! No one should ever go through this, and it's being done to eight billion chickens a year in the U.S. alone. Now do you know what that means?"

I guess I looked confused because he continues explaining.

"Eight billion is an unimaginable number, right? Let's put it in more understandable terms, shall we? Mmmm…" Romeo scratches his head with the tip of his wing as he thinks. "Okay, 10 billion bricks were used to build the Empire State building. So you throw in the amount of chickens that are eaten in Puerto Rico and the Caribbean, and you've got a skyscraper of dead chickens!" He now shrills madly.

Romeo's anger is burning out of control like a wildfire in a forest during a drought. He starts to cluck loudly while wildly flapping his wings. I jump back, just in time before he gets too close to whacking my knees.

"Pardon my language but I seethe with righteous indignation and tend to get carried away. I'm now officially in a melancholy mood. That's all I'm saying about the fate of my feathered friends." He grumbles as he turns and walks away, muttering to himself, "For someone with no voice, she sure asks a lot of questions."

I didn't —I can't! — ask anything! What's he talking about? He now shrills madly. I want to comfort him. I want to comfort a rooster! He looks mad, upset, and so sad. I don't do anything. I don't know what to do, but I do take my notes. I take lots and lots of notes. I organize my bag and act a little busy. I then adjust my 'perch' position as a calmer looking Romeo comes back.

"Where's my Miss Honey? It's been a while. OH, here is Janet — one of my wives.

"*Yoo-hoo* Janet, my love, this is our Reporter..."

I nod and smile hello, but Janet doesn't seem to be interested in me.

Romeo puts his wing around Janet and asks, "Would you mind doing me a huge favor and checking on Miss Honey? She went beyond the fence about a half hour ago to gather some fresh clover. Please don't *you* leave Animal Haven, just ask around if any of the others know her whereabouts for me, darling. Thank you, love." Romeo blows Janet a kiss as she nods sweetly and struts away.

"Janet, what a sweetheart, she's one of the Katrina chickens. Have you heard about them?"

I shake my head no.

"In 2005, after Hurricane Katrina hit, we rescued close to 1,000 chicks raised as broiler chickens.

"Come on, let's walk to the east wing of the chicken barn where the Katrina chickens live,"

114

Romeo says while offering me his wing to hold. "It might be meditation time.

"The senior chickens moved my families, as well as myself, to the west wing. I enjoy singing and cock-a-doodling too early. According to them, some of the older chickens complained. They like to sleep late — like to the crack of noon some of them — and they call themselves chickens! Ha!

"I still wake up and 'do my thing.' I usually take a short walk to the cow barn first. Miss Honey is up early, and we go for walks while... umm... planning the day's events on the farm." He quickly glances in my direction.

Uh-huh, "planning!" I smile at him.

"So, the Katrina chickens, besides being traumatized from experiencing the nightmare of the hurricane and the lack of rescue efforts afterwards, were also subjected to unnatural breeding at their farm. They were bred to grow twice as fast and twice as large, like super chickens. The demand for more meat, in less time, to make more money; that's what it all comes down to - money!

"Some of the disturbed roosters joined gangs and were even killing the hens. Chickens, as I might have mentioned, are *good* social birds. They do not kill. They just don't! These few foul fowl had to be separated from the rest of us because of this unnatural violent behavior. Its nature verses nurture, and these guys had the worst of both. They couldn't help who they became!

"Many of our Katrina friends have passed away from sickness because of weight-related health problems. Some of them had ligament, joint, and foot infections. Others had rickets. Some even died from sudden death syndrome. Many of them had been genetically altered to eat too much in order to grow excessively fast. A number of them impulsively ate straw or other strange things that stuck in their digestive tracts and caused blockages, which led to infection. A few of these disturbed chickens were even eating excrement!" he says with a look of revulsion on his face. "Again, not their fault," Romeo says holding his wing up.

"Our friends received around-the-clock medical care here. Most of the chickens needed years of counseling, and some are still in it. Besides physical ailments, they're still suffering emotionally from survivors' guilt."

We reach a small modern addition added onto the larger barn. I stop and stoop down to read a schedule sheet posted on a bulletin board of the east wing barn's door. Umm... oh wow, aside from yoga, they have tap, ballet, and… nice, they have Zumba classes on Monday nights. 'The Fab Foul' will be performing in a show next weekend, singing songs from their 'Set it Free' album. Umm, Sheryl Crow, at the end of the month, and…

"Here, look," Romeo calls me over with a wing wave. "Erica, our exercise instructor, is having a *Poultry-in-Motion* class right now. It's a lot like yoga with light stretching and bending."

Did he say…? He opens the barn door and I hear —

"Stretch your wings to the sky ladies, and hold — two, three, and release, and let's repeat … stretch and hold — two, three … great job! Now we are going to do some forward bends. We were working on them yesterday. Don't forget to inhale through your nose, pause, and exhale through your beaks. Ready and…" then Erica stops.

All eyes are on me! Yep, a dozen or so chickens in yoga pants are staring at me! I grin shyly and then look down and shuffle my feet. Nothing in life prepares you for smiling and trying to be accepted by a flock of birds — except maybe that time in middle school during the science fair when I was asked a question and – no, no, no – this is worse. Right then the exercise music speeds up a

notch. I'm so self-conscious that a knee-jerk reaction
takes over my mind and body and I start doing the
chicken dance! I hear muffled cackling and clucking
— but do I stop? No, I can't!

Romeo gives me his wing at the appropriate
'swing-your-partner' time — I try to take it, but he
forcefully leads me out of the barn while nodding and
mumbling apologies. I hear Erica and the flock of
yoga chicken-ladies explode with a loud cackling
laughter as we leave. My burning embarrassment
spurts out of my face and runs down my body like hot
lava as we leave.

Romeo narrows his eyes, turns his head staring
up at me, and then he chokes out a half cock-a-
doodle-do and half laugh ...

"A reporter with a sense of humor, I like that,"
Romeo nods, still giggling. "Thanks, the girls really
needed a good release, and I guess I did too.
Laughter is the best medicine, and one can never get
enough of that in one's life, no?

You're quite welcome. I am SO glad I can help.
I try to brush off my humiliation and act as if I meant
to do that little dance.

"As you see, the one thing I find truly incredible
about these gals is that most of them are still cheerful

after all they've been through. Many have even been healthy enough to leave.

"My Janet was one of the many of thousands that were being bulldozed into a large pit. It was during the 'clean up' after the hurricane. It was easier and cheaper for them just to dispose of all the chickens — dead, injured, sick, and alive. Janet, found struggling to survive, was gutsy but as fragile as a new butterfly," Romeo recalls with a smile. "More courageous than most and such a determined will to live! My poor darling had severe gangrene and had to have half of her foot removed. She has a permanent limp, but she is still a beauty. I think she can still strut her stuff even with that shuffle in her walk," he says with a wink-wink expression. "It took her months to get acclimated to this decadent lifestyle at Animal Haven. Such a mess she was on the night she came here. I remember that night as if it were yesterday. The second our eyes met, I fell in love again, for the twelfth time, I believe. Oh, that evening…" I watch his gaze travel back in time. Romeo then flaps up onto the fence, clears his throat, and begins:

> *"Some enchanted evening*
> *You may see a chicken,*

you may see a chicken
Across a crowded barn"

He's singing! Is he really belting out a tune from
that old movie South Pacific?

"And somehow you know,
You know she's your hen
That somewhere you'll see her
Again and again.
Some enchanted evening…"

Now I am starting to feel a little bit
uncomfortable. Do I smile? Where should I put my
hands? I start to sway to the song, but that doesn't
feel right. So I stop and shuffle my feet a little bit. I
can feel "the giggles" coming on. I can't laugh! I can't
laugh, I can't laugh! He seems to be in a trance.
You're not supposed to interrupt someone in a
trance, right? Or is that sleepwalking? Is he going to
sing the whole song? I can't take this another second
– I AM going to laugh!

"…When you find another true love,
When you hear her cluck at you
Across a crowded barn,

120

Then FLY to her side,
And make her your own
For all through your life you
May dream all alone.
Once you have found her,
Never let her go.
Once you have found her,
Never let her gooooooo!"

He stops singing, but he still has that romantic glazed look in his eyes. I don't trust myself not to laugh, so I force my face to freeze in a smile. Should I clap? That's it - maybe he's waiting for applause. Yeah, I'll clap really loud to get his attention – and because he did sing beautifully.

I clap once, and then I clap a few more times a little harder, which makes him jump a little. Romeo shakes his head and looks at me. It seems to have interrupted his reverie. I sure hope he's calmer now.

"I am *so* sorry. I tend to get caught up in my memories and break into song. It's a bad habit, but it's better than gambling – which I am NOT going to talk about! Again, I *do* apologize!"

He suddenly stops, looks closely at my fake frozen smile that I still have plastered on my face, and asks, "Why are you smiling like that, Reporter?

You look a little ill. Are you okay?" He reaches over to feel my forehead with the back of his wing.

'I'm all right,' I try to say as I jump back a bit, but I end up just giving him a thumbs-up. And then I start a self-conscious 'high five,' which I quickly decide to stop (because of the hand-wing confusion), and end up pushing my hair out of my eyes. Did I just do a strange version of the Macarena dance? Thank goodness, Janet appears.

"Here she is — my Janet." She whispers something to Romeo while nodding. "So you DID see Miss Honey, and she's now going for wild flowers? Thank you my love, thank you!"

I smile with a head nod. Before she leaves, he pecks her on the beak and she pecks him back, affectionately. I don't want to interrupt so I turn slowly, then give Janet a friendly look and shrug my shoulders as she walks away. I hope she doesn't think that I'm trying to steal her rooster.

Janet struts "her stuff" away with an air of indifference.

Motioning with a wave of his wing, Romeo invites me to follow. "Let's go take a walk, and I'll introduce you so some of the pigs here. Today is a gift, now isn't it? Look at the blue skies! Do you smell that sweetness in the air? I just love these Indian summer days!"

It is a lovely day. The bright rising sun is finally up high enough in the sky and is warming the air already. The air smells clean and fresh. I think about my dear friend Miss Honey and wonder what she's doing. She has been gone for a long time. I hope she's okay.

Romeo and I walk a little through an open field. A gentle breeze begins to blow, making the golden confetti of falls leaves dance around us. I stop and look around me. This place is beautiful! I take a deep breath, close my eyes, and let the warm November morning's sun bathe my new spirit. I let the surreal events of the day seep into my pores. I open my eyes refreshed with a newfound energy as I notice a few bunnies skip past. They stop, wiggle their noses, and grin at me. They are just so cute! I squat down to pet them and the littlest bunny hops onto my lap cuddling up to me 'ahhing' and 'cooing.' I relish the feel of her bunny kisses on my cheeks. A bigger bunny looks up and says "Come on Rosie, mama is waiting." Rosie hops off and then they all leap away happily giggling and smiling. She turns around to wave at me. I smile as I think; all the animals look so peaceful and happy living here.

THE POND

"Ready to go?" Romeo asks. "I really need a brisk walk to ruffle off this anxious mood I'm feeling. I'm worried about Miss Honey. It is a dangerous world out there on the outside. There is just so much one Rooster can do in these circumstances. They say I'm moody, but it's just that, I don't know, maybe I know too much?" he says with a haughty headshake.

I get up looking around for more bunnies before I go. Romeo takes my arm with his wing while leading me to the path. He is such a gentlemen, and I am enjoying his attentiveness. I can understand why his ladies swoon over him, although I do sense an egotistical tone in some of his remarks, but I'm not a hen. Haha! Maybe all roosters are this – cock-sure. I chuckle at my pun.

"Pigs — I can't say anything *bad* about a pig! You know how dogs seem to love people a bit too unconditionally, and cats are very independent and tend to be moody." He says, choosing his words carefully, "Some days you might owe *them* an apology for something as simple as feeding them moist food on Monday? And, I think, some of them have such arrogant attitudes too." He shakes his head smiling. "But pigs, they treat you, no matter *who* you are, as an equal. If someone should call you a pig, say '*thank you.*' It IS a huge compliment, honestly! In my opinion, pigs usually seem to get a bad rap these days. People tend to think of them as dirty or dumb. That is actually a myth. Pigs are smart, affectionate, and very clean. I hope I won't seem presumptuous if I offer you some advice. Here's my tip," Romeo says, as if he's telling me a secret. "If you want to fall in love with a pig, look him straight in the eyes; you will fall in love with him instantly, just like magic!

"Farmer Harry says that pigs have eyes like humans. We get to see what they're feeling deep into their souls just by looking into their eyes. They also make very good friends," he adds nodding.

As I think about pigs, it dawns on me that I've eaten pigs in the past. I've never called my meals "flesh of a pig" before but I've referred to it as "pork" or "ham," and to me, that has made it edible and guilt-free. Could it be that it's called a different name to remove fact from reality? No remorse eating "a pork," right? Pork isn't an animal. Actually, it is — it's a pig! I think of bacon and instantly drool. I love the taste of bacon. A holiday ham, a ham sandwich – it's all pig? I don't think I would have eaten a "loin of pig" or "pulled pig," right? I rub my achy and confused head.

Same with beef, that's not the name of an animal either — it's cow! What if the word "cow" was used instead of "steak" or "beef" while ordering it at restaurant? "I'd like my flank-cow rare, please, still a little bloody, with a side order of fries..." I start to gag, but the sight of a large duck in the distance distracts me.

"Here's the pond and it's Danny!" Romeo waves his wing excitedly, shouting. "How are you today?

"Danny, the duck, he's the lifeguard at the pond on his days off. He's saved many lives, he has!" Romeo quickly fills me in on this information as the duck waddles closer to us. "He works at Cornell University hospital a few days a week, too. He's a Cayuga duck. See how big and broad-shouldered he is? A well-built drake — the ladies flock to him. A good down-to-earth guy he is."

Danny the duck waltzes over and greets us waving the life preserver that he's carrying. He's a strong, good-looking duck covered with greenish-tinted black feathers.

"Romeo, my man, I'm doing well. Give me some feather. How you doin'? And how about your families?" Danny says, lifting his sunglasses to the top of his head to get a better look at me.

"Great, we are absolutely fine," Romeo boasts, raising his beak slightly. "Clementine's eggs just hatched on Thursday. We now have three new baby chicks." He smiles, "Oh, my darling, *oh my darling, oh my darling Clementine…*" Romeo begins to sing.

Uh-oh…here he goes again!

"THAT IS WONDERFUL news Romeo. REALLY, it is …" Danny answers a little too enthusiastically while giving Romeo an extra hard congratulatory whack on his back with his wing — which breaks the musical mood and ends Romeo's singing.

A good save by a duck — I like him already!

"So, what can I help you with today? I know you don't like to swim, and I see you have a visitor today. Giving a tour?" asks Danny as he nods in my direction with a wink.

"Yes, this is 'Reporter' and she wants to interview the animals and write a story about us at Animal Haven. We're on our way to see the pigs right now."

Danny flashes me a toothless, mischievous Cheshire cat grin and holds up his wing to high "feather" me. I reciprocate and high feather him back. I try to act hip, as if I've done this before. Be cool. Keep it lookin' cool.

"You just missed Enzo," Danny says, still smiling. "Those pigs sure love to swim just as much as they love rolling in the mud. It cools them off. Smart guy, that Enzo...," Danny flexes his big, strong wing in my direction. "Actually, all of these pigs are smart! Did you know that they rate the fourth smartest animal after chimpanzees, dolphins, and elephants? Enzo was reading *The Wall St. Journal*, but he had to leave to bring in fresh hay for tomorrow's feast."

Jeez, I missed Enzo! He sure loves to hang out with the animals.

Romeo looks at his watch (his watch?) and suddenly seems distracted and anxious. "Danny, would you do me a favor and explain your position at the Cornwell Animal University to Reporter? Then would you kindly please point her in the direction towards the pig barn if I'm not back?

"There's just one tiny, umm issue," Romeo whispers turning his back slightly away from me. "Reporter can't speak..."

128

Hello! I can't speak but I can still hear!

"She lost her voice. If you happen to see it —
what does 'a voice' look like, anyway? She's okay
though — safe, but a bit strange, in an amusing way.
My Miss Honey has been gone for a long time, and
I'm getting worried. I will not be longer than two
shakes of a lamb's tail. THANKS!" Romeo waves as
he rushes quickly away, not giving Danny any time to
reply to his request.

I wave and smile and — goodness — did I just
bow? "Strange," did he say? Thanks a lot! I shouldn't
feel insulted that I've just been dumped by a rooster,
but he should go looking for Miss Honey. She has
been gone a very long time.

So, I've chatted with a turkey and a rooster. I
can certainly handle a duck! I smile again. I have to
stop smiling. I try to put on a mock serious face, but it
feels awkward. Let me just be...natural? How have I
behaved around ducks in the past? Huh?

"Nice to meet you, Reporter. Word on the farm
is that Romeo and Miss Honey are in *love*," he says,
sarcastically emphasizing the word and ending it with
a kiss sound. "But they won't admit it. Are you picking
up on those love vibes too?"

I smile, yet again! I nod my head in agreement. This duck is rather hip, perceptive — and very charming too.

"Everyone sees it. Quite the scandal that'll make: a duck and a turkey. Aha! That Romeo, he's okay though, a bit of a maverick, but he gets things done around here. Are you enjoying your tour at Animal Haven? Nice place we have, huh?"

I nod as I point around the farm with my arms. We take a few steps, and Danny suddenly stops and turns to me.

"To be quite honest, I've heard about you," Danny says with a knowing look. "News spreads quickly around here." He pauses, choosing his words carefully, "I'd like to thank you in advance for helping us." With a slight bow of his head, he takes my hand in his wing and kisses it. Right then five little ducks waddle by. "Pardon me," Danny says releasing my hand. "HEY, little ducklings, NO roughhousing at the pond today. Where's your mother?"

A large looking battered duck waves her wing from across the pond and shouts: **"Danny, I am over here. Sorry. Ducklings, I warned you before we got here! Now behave or we're going home!"**

"Cathy, my dear, I didn't know they were yours. They're just having some fun. Don't you worry!"

"Thanks, Danny. I can't look away for a second without one of them getting into something! Little Dotty...what did I just say?"

"Ducklings will be ducklings, Cathy." Danny yells back. He then turns and whispers, "Did you hear her rough, raspy voice? Cathy was a *foie gras* duck, which translates into 'fatty liver' in French. There are a few others like her here, and they all sound the same. One goose insisted that her name was '*Pâté*' when she arrived here. We ended up calling her 'Patty,'" he says rolling his eyes.

I shake my head because I don't understand.

He continues, "The *foie gras* ducks and geese have gone through unimaginable pain and a psychologically terrorizing ordeal before they were rescued and brought here. You see, they were brutally force-fed many times a day. An 8 to 12-inch pipe was shoved down their throats at the *foie gras* factories for up to 18 days before their slaughter time. Their fattened livers grow to become 10 times larger than their normal size. The livers, which are usually diseased, become high priced hors d'oeuvres for people. It's barbaric what our animal friends on the outside suffer to become food for people. Who even *thinks* of these sick practices?" He asks, shuddering.

131

I've heard of it before. I've never eaten it. I've never even thought much of it — but Cathy? She seems like such a sweet duck, a typical mother with babies! Did he say a 12-inch pipe shoved down her throat?! Why is this torture even legal?

"Farmer Harry and other activists have worked so hard to have laws passed to stop this cruel 'delicacy.' Some states have already banned these sick practices recently. Many famous chefs have also been voicing their opinions to stop this ritual."

What's the deal with this guy? Why is he so sweet? That Farmer Harry has done so much for the animals. What a humanitarian, good for him!

A big beach ball flies past our faces, and Danny says, "These teenaged ducks now a day, would you look at them in the pond?" Then he shouts, "'C'MON GUYS, take it easy, ducklings are in the pond today!" He turns to me with a grin and says, "They don't know how lucky they are! Aha! *Lucky ducks!*" He chuckles at his joke, sticking out his tongue and making a goofy expression.

"So, my job, I work at Cornell University Hospital. I'm a volunteer blood donor there. When a sick duck arrives needing my help, they call me in to assist. I truly enjoy what I do. It's my gift of love, you'd say. After I'm done, I like to walk around the campus and hang with the wild geese and ducks. What a treat *that* is. I love it! So totally cool…they have a one-of-a-kind sense of humor—such pranksters, some of them! Do you hear them honking all the time? They're actually laughing. I always leave there in a fine mood," says Danny, flashing me his trademark smile.

Yes, I've heard that honking sound before! I thought they sounded happy —but laughing? That's surprising!

Danny cuts short my thoughts with a wave of his large black wing. "The sun is out; this warm weather is going to bring the crowds out real soon. How about I take an early break and accompany you to the pig barn?

"Nathan, Nick, and Gene just got here to cover me. Those two ducks and the goose are best of friends…"

Duck, duck, goose — HA-HA!

"I don't know their stories, but they're always together, and such animal activists they are!

"Hey my three amigos, I'll be back after my break. Watch those ducks, will ya please?"

"NO problem, Danny," the three honk in unison. "Thanks!"

133

"Have you met my good friend, Jack-Lucas the goat, yet?" Danny asks.

I shake my head no.

"Jack-Lucas should be hanging out with the other goats his age around this time of day. We met at the animal hospital. Poor little guy, he's such a trooper. Did you know that there are over one hundred live-kill markets in the New York City area alone? Occasionally, a brave soul runs for his life from those markets. Some make it, most don't. In fact, some of them live here at Animal Haven. Jack-Lucas was one of the lucky ones. They found him wandering around a park in Brooklyn. He was dangerously underweight and malnourished. His mouth and nose were infected with ORF disease, that's a zoonotic virus, which means that it can be contagious to humans. It's a very painful abrasion condition for sheep and goats. That's probably why he was so tiny, it was too painful to eat. This little guy also had an infected leg from being tightly hog-tied. That's a common way to carry goats to the slaughterhouse. A big chunk of his hoof fell off 'cause of lack of circulation. His mouth healed eventually, but his hoof wound was so severe that his leg had to be amputated above the knee," Danny says wincing as he makes a cutting motion on his leg with his wing.

"That's when I met him at the hospital. He was in the recovery room. I sat with him and told him all about his new home at Animal Haven. We joke now about it, but he thought I was lying just to make him feel better. I had such a tough job understanding him back then. He has a squeaky voice and used to have a thick *'New Yawk'* accent, he'd call it. He'd say 'Fuhgeddaboutit,' instead of 'forget about it.' And 'Pahrmee' for 'Pardon me.' And..." Danny chuckles as he remembers, "it took us days to figure out that 'Nyes-plays-ha-gottere' meant: 'Nice place you got here.'"

My mouth is hanging open, and I didn't even realize it! A bug flies in it; I cough and spit it out. I'm amazed, sad, and happy all at the same time by everything this little goat has endured. What a story!

"Did you know that goats can change their way of speaking, or their accent, if they hang out with a new group of goats for a while? Totally cool! Betcha you can't do that! Aha, just joking with ya." Danny pokes me as he remembers about my lost voice. "C'mon, we're almost there," he says, guiding me with his wing.

"Jack-Lucas had *some* medical bills. *Cha-ching, cha-ching!* His good friend, Mr. Martin Rowe, such an amazing guy, ran his first 26-mile marathon in New York City and raised $11,000 to help with the bills. Can you beat that? It quacks me to tears just to think how above and beyond some nice people truly are. Jack-Lucas now has a prosthetic leg, and he's healthy. He hangs out with the other goats and sheep, as I said. They get in trouble sometimes making a mess with the food bins, but it's all harmless fun."

I stretch my head and look around. I want to meet Jack-Lucas! I have to meet this goat before I leave. Leave? What if I can't leave? What if I'm here, with no voice, forever! What if …

"Yeah, those goats are a fun-lovin' group. You know how you human folk have the expression, *'Dance like no one is watching?'* That's how goats live their lives. They have fun for the sake of having fun. Just watch them run and gallop and prance around in the pastures." Danny chuckles. "Frolickers, they are! They always make me smile. If they had hair on their heads it would always be down and blowing in the wind. Also, their personalities are as individualistic as all the doctors at the hospital are. Nah, they *have* more personalities than the doctors do, aha! But you didn't hear that from me," he says with a wink and a slight nudge with his wing.

"Some goats are shy. They like to get to know you better before they warm up, just like humans. Some are mischievous, playful, and downright goofy! Occasionally, they can get themselves in real trouble with their intelligence, curiosity, AND high-energy levels. Hey, sometimes I want to tell them just to sit down and chill out for a while.

"Unfortunately, these fun-lovin,' good-hearted guys are the most eaten animal flesh in the world. It disturbs me to tell you about it because too many of my friends are goats."

Goats? Who eats goats? I've known of goat cheese and goat milk but never thought of ever eating goat meat, though. But people eat goats?

"So, to tie my life up in a bow, that's pretty much my story. When I'm not there at the hospital, I'm here at the pond. Life is good, my friend. Life IS good.

"The pigs live just up over the hill to the left. Watch your step, Reporter, poop happens — and it happens a lot around here."

Whoooa, that was a big pile. Good thing I wore my old sneakers!

"JUST THE FACTS"

"We'll be passing the cow barn on the way. I hope our heifers, the famous trio, didn't leave for the pastures yet. They like to relax under the trees to keep out of the heat on these warm days.

"I'm sure they've been busy for weeks now, decorating the big barn for tomorrow's festivities," Danny explains. "That's our venue for gatherings. First the turkeys parade in, all bedecked in flowers. What a grand entrance! We all serve the turkeys when they're settled, and then we all eat! Oh, the music and dancing – it's a grand time!"

"My feisty ladies, Tori, Charlene, and Cheyenne," Danny smiles. "Those heifers have fascinating rescue stories. Actually, they're all runaways.

"I don't know what happened to Romeo," he rolls his eyes laughing. "Between you, me, and the lamb's toes, he's probably serenading his hens right now.

"The cow barn is right over here. C'mon. Watch your step, again."

138

There's no missing the party barn with the hand-dipped, silver glittered fall foliage outlining the entrance. The path to the door is lined with beautiful arrangements of golden mums and sunflowers. Danny gives a friendly whistle through his wing feathers and sings out:

"Torrrri! Where are you? It's Danny...and we have a vis-i-tor."

Just then an enormous brown and white spotty cow saunters from behind the barn and says:

"Hey, Danny, I haven't seen you in a ... in a blue *mooooon.* I was just thinking about you today too. Isn't the weather a treat for this time of year? A gift I tell you — a gift! Between the gorgeous day and excitement for tomorrow's festivities, everyone's in such grand spirits."

"Yes, Tori, it *is* beautiful! I know the pond is going to get crowded today. I expect they'll all be out soon. I can't stay long. We're on our way to interview the pigs."

"How's work, Danny? Busy?"

"I have no complaints, Tori. Are you here all alone? Where are the other ladies?"

"I told Charlee and Cheyenne to go to the pastures and relax. I was just putting the finishing floral touches on the barn for tomorrow's Thanks-

Living feast. I get more accomplished by myself sometimes. I'd jump over the moon for those two, and I love them like sistas, but they sure love to chew the cud… and, oh!" Tori says suddenly glancing at me. "I'm sorry, who's this new face?"

"This is 'Reporter,'" Danny says, and noticing my nervousness, he nudges me with his wing to move closer. "She's the one who's been taking notes on the animals at Animal Haven this morning. She doesn't speak, though. Romeo said she lost her voice," Danny adds with a wing shrug.

I try to convey my apologies with a hand motion, but Danny keeps on explaining as we walk into the barn.

SQUEAK!

"I have to get that door oiled! If you close it real gently, it's not that noisy," explains Tori.

"Welcome to my humble abode," she says as she steps aside to let me enter first.

WOW! I'm taken back by how pretty it is inside — it's breathtaking! I feel as if I've been transported to another world, certainly nothing I've ever seen on a farm before. The white twinkling lights that frame the interior of the barn give it a chic, yet a festive atmosphere. Centerpieces of miniature crowns of roses and baby's breath (I assume for the turkeys to

140

wear) displayed on the banquet-size tables are dressed in colorful leaves and flowers, and…oh my, is that a dance floor in the middle? I walk off and nosey around by myself while Danny and Tori chat.

"We're having a story written about us," I hear Danny explain, glancing in my direction. He thinks for a second and says, "I have an idea. I know you're busy, but do you have a few minutes, Tori? Now, *you* have a great story to share."

"Oh, stop Danny!" Tori smiles, nodding in agreement, "But it's true, I love my story and I absolutely adore telling it. I still get cow bumps. I must admit— it is a mooving tale."

BRRRAAAPP!

I jump up and swing around knocking into a large platter that crashes loudly off the table. What was that? Did Tori just pass gas?

Tori pauses and gives me a look of annoyance.

Now I'm embarrassed that I might have embarrassed her. I try peeking at her from the corner of my eye, but she doesn't seem to mind anymore and continues speaking. Perhaps, bodily functions are accepted here. When in Rome…?

"I have had many adventures in the days before I came here," Tori responds happily as if rediscovering a treasure from the past. "Sure, come

141

over here and sit down, Reporter, before you wreck the place," she adds grumbling under her breath. "I still need to arrange these flowers anyway, and maybe you can help me while we chat. Yes, that's what we'll do! See you tomorrow, Danny! Enjoy the day!"

It takes me a second before I realize that Tori has called my name. I see Danny move towards the door. I wave and mouth, *Bye Danny, thank you!* He turns back around gives me a thumb up — umm, how does he do that with his feathers?

"Show Reporter the way to the pigs when you are finished, please. See ya! Thanks. Nice chatting with you, dear lady. Good luck with your book." He shouts over his shoulder giving me a wink.

I wave again as Danny leaves and chuckle at the thought: my book! How did this rumor get started in the first place? *My book...* I get chills of excitement from the thought. Sure, I'll write a story about my adventures here. I can —

"Ahem..." Tori clears her throat, "So, YOU are the Reporter?' I've heard about you from one of the chickens, Janet, I think it was. I'll give you my story, but I have to share with you that I do *not* like people. Let me rephrase that. I don't *trust* you people. I'm a little nervous around them too. My counselor says my mistrust is because of what I've been through. I am working on it, though," she says eyeing me suspiciously. "People have to earn my trust. Please don't take it personally and please know that I'm very glad you are writing about the farm. It's a great idea, actually!"

BURRPP!

Tori nods my, "Excuuuse me!"

I jump. I'm a little nervous. I'm sitting here with this huge cow who is in counseling, she has a digestive problem and is admitting to me that she doesn't like people AND she wants me to help her with her arts and crafts project — there are just so many things wrong with this scene!

"Now Reporter, before I begin my tale, I'm going to explain a little something about us cows. I notice that you seem a bit…disgusted? Shocked? What I have to say may make you somewhat uncomfortable. It's not pleasant…" Tori says holding up a hoof, "but it is, what it is!"

I look at Tori waiting anxiously for her to continue. Oh no, maybe she's angry, and is going reprimand me for eating hamburgers. Okay, used to eat them. I don't anymore, but she doesn't know that. How am I going to explain? I smile at her nervously and gesture for her to continue. I'm ready to hear this…

"We have gas!" Tori blurts out.

I gasp and cover my mouth in shock at first and then all of a sudden I feel that I'm going to laugh! I feel those out-of-control giggles coming on again, and I try to shake it off as the tears are building up. I can't laugh. No, I can't laugh! Quick, think of something sad: sickness, war, lives of the chickens…something - anything to neutralize my sudden giddiness. This cow is going to get insulted if I laugh in her face. She's about to share with me something personal; she's going to tell me about her gas problems!

She turns and looks away before continuing. "It's not your occasional little polite *toot,* but how can I say this?" She twists her face thinking, "It's rip-roaring gas — and, it's lethal. Should I use the word 'flatulence,' or would that be rude? Oops, I just did," Tori says covering her mouth with her hoof.

Did this cow just say "flatulence?" Don't laugh, don't laugh, don't laugh…

"The cows here at Animal Haven, are much healthier because our diets have improved, but when we first got here — holy cow! The other cows and I thought we could blow the roof off this barn due to our problem. How can I explain this? Let's just say that the peace and the tranquility of the 'pastures of pleasures' are usually overcome by the *symphony of nature*. Are you getting the picture, Reporter? Point being, I am not going to excuse myself every single time I do a ...*faux pas*. Umm, I wonder if that's what the French cows call it. And the belching..." she nods, "we do a lot of that too."

I smile politely. I keep my mouth covered to muffle the laughter and hold my nose waiting for a strong breeze to clear the air. 'Symphony of nature?' Faux Pas? I'm going to burst out laughing. "Burst out" — like a cow! Don't laugh, don't laugh, don't laugh...

"Enzo read about our condition and told us recently that it's not our fault. It's just the way life is for us. We always were and always will be very gassy animals. I still couldn't quite understand all of this information, it's quite scientific, Enzo gave me this article..." She awkwardly gets up and lifts a large box from under the table.

How nice is that Enzo to educate the animals? Nice ... but odd.

"I have it here someplace...now where is ...?" Tori mumbles, rummaging through scraps of craft papers, ribbons, and newspaper clippings in a carton that's labeled *STUFF*.

"That Enzo, he gets around," Tori stops her hunt and faces me. "He has recently gone to see a new documentary in New York City called, *Cowspiracy*." She shakes her head and laughs. "He's become quite good friends with the producer, Kip Anderson. Amazing film Enzo said, genius! Scary though… but, people have to know. They have to know and they have to do something, now!" She sighs loudly, sadly, as she continues with her search more desperately.

"Here it is! It's just the facts from the *Cowspiracy* documentary. He and I have discussed it on occasion. You can have it. I'm not much of a reader. The thing that I don't understand is," Tori says sadly, "that it just seems, so wrong! So *very* wrong, on so many levels, but that's just my opinion, and I'm just a cow. Maybe I'm the stupid one, I don't know. It *has* to be the right thing if the people — if the government — is doing it, right?

I shrug my shoulders. I guess so.

"Let me explain, from the beginning — blow by blow," she says, smirking slowly after realizing what she just said. "Human folk in the United States eat three times more beef than people in any other country, and that adds up to roughly three hamburgers per person every week. That comes to about 48 billion burgers eaten in this country a year. I'm surprised you guys aren't mooing yet...," Tori pauses and looks at me for a moment, waiting for me to comment, "...ya know, since you all eat so much beef!"

I smile and nod. She is right.

"Livestock takes up 30% percent of the earth's land. That's us animals and all the land that it takes to produce food *just* for us to eat. Seventy percent of grains and cereals that are grown in this country are food for farmed animals. Can you imagine how many starving people in this country that would feed? In addition, can you comprehend how much land you would have to grow fruit and vegetables? Whatsa matter, you human folks don't like that stuff?"

'I do,' I want to say, so I nod. I eat my quota — what is it, one or two servings a week? Or should it be a day? Yeah, whatever — I'm sure I eat enough.

"Did you know that it takes, more or less, one thousand gallons of water just to make one hamburger?"

I write '1,000 gallons of water to make one hamburger.' Really?! I put up my hand for her to stop talking. I'm not quite sure I understand — this is all

147

crazy! Let me just take my notes, and I'll google all my information when I go home.

"You might be wondering why it takes so much land and water to feed a cow? Well, I'll tell ya. Look at me. Cows are big animals, and we eat a lot of food! Before the 1970s we ate mostly grass, but this country decided that it would be more economical to feed us corn, grains and..." she gulps, "by-products." She bugs out her eyes and says, "I'll tell you about that later. Therefore, they feed us this new diet to *help* us grow faster so they can kill us sooner. Not that we're fussy about what we eat or anything, but cows are ruminants, which mean we have rumens. That's the part of our stomach used to break down gases. We are supposed to eat a lot of grass - roughage. If we don't get enough, we develop lactic acid in our rumens, and it creates even more gas than we normally would have. The gas - not a big deal, you'd think, except for embarrassing moments at social events, right? Wrong!" Tori straightens out her paper and waves it in front of me. "Enzo says that our belching and flatulence issue is the main cause for the greenhouse gases that are causing all this pollution. Animal agriculture contributes an extremely large percentage of the greenhouse gases worldwide – more than planes, trains, and automobiles, combined! Here, take a look at this paper," she says as she hands it to me.

I take the paper from Tori and glance at it. It's titled Cowspiracy: Just the Facts.

"Make yourself comfortable and read it," she says. "Go on..."

Cowspiracy: Just the Facts

• Animal agriculture is responsible for 18 percent of greenhouse gas emissions, more than all transportation combined.

• Transportation is responsible for 13% of all greenhouse gas emissions.

• Livestock and their byproducts actually account for at least 32,000 million tons of carbon dioxide (CO2) per year, or 51% of all worldwide greenhouse gas emissions.

• Methane is 25-100 times more destructive than CO2.

• Methane has a global warming power 86 times that of CO2.

• Livestock is responsible for 65% of all emissions of nitrous oxide – a greenhouse gas 296x more destructive than carbon dioxide and which stays in the atmosphere for 150 years.

• Animal agriculture use ranges from 34-76 trillion gallons of water annually.

149

- Agriculture is responsible for 80-90% of US water consumption.

- Growing feed crops for livestock consumes 56% of water in the US.

- One hamburger requires 660 gallons of water to produce – the equivalent of 2 months' worth of showers.

- 2,500 gallons of water are needed to produce 1 pound of beef.

- 477 gallons of water are required to produce 1 pound of eggs; 900 gallons of water are needed for cheese.

- 1,000 gallons of water are required to produce 1 gallon of milk.

- 5% of water in the US is used by private homes. 55% of water in the US is used for animal agriculture.

- The meat and dairy industries combined use nearly 1/3 (29%) of all the fresh water in the world today.

- Livestock covers 45% of the earth's total land.

- Animal agriculture is the leading cause of species extinction, ocean dead zones, water pollution and habitat destruction.

- Every minute, 7 million pounds of excrement are produced by animals raised for food in the US.
This doesn't include the animals raised outside of USDA jurisdiction or in backyards, or the billions of fish raised in aquaculture settings in the US.

150

- A farm with 2,500 dairy cows produces the same amount of waste as a city of 411,000 people.
- Animal agriculture is responsible for 91% of Amazon destruction.
- 1-2 acres of rainforest are cleared every second.
- The leading causes of rainforest destruction are livestock and feed-crops.
- 110 plant, animal and insect species are lost every day 136-million rainforest acres cleared for animal agriculture due to rainforest destruction.
- 1,100 activists have been killed in Brazil in the past 20 years.
- Cows produce 150 billion gallons of methane per day
- 130 times more animal waste than human waste is produced in the US – 1.4 billion tons from the meat industry annually. 5 tons of animal waste is produced for every person.
- 2-5 acres of land are used per cow.
- The average American consumes 209 pounds of meat per year.
- Nearly half of the contiguous US is devoted to animal agriculture.
30% of the Earth's entire land surface is used by the livestock sector.
- 1/3 of the planet is desertified due to livestock.

151

- 70 billion farmed animals are reared annually worldwide. More than 6 million animals are killed for food every hour.

- Land required to feed 1 person for 1 year:

Vegan: 1/6th acre

Vegetarian: 3x as much as a vegan

Meat Eater: 18x as much as a vegan

- 1.5 acres can produce 37,000 pounds of plant-based food.

1.5 acres can produce 375 pounds of meat.

- A person who follows a vegan diet uses 50% less carbon dioxide, 1/11th oil, 1/13th water, and 1/18th land compared to a meat-eater.

- Each day, a person who eats a vegan diet saves 1,100 gallons of water, 45 pounds of grain, 30 sq ft of forested land, 20 lbs CO2 equivalent, and one animal's life.

I put the paper on my lap and sit there in a daze. Tori stares at me for a reaction; I have none. I'm not sure if I understand what this all means. This is heavy stuff. I wonder if I'll get a visit from the CIA for knowing all this top secret information. They'll bug my phone and monitor my every move. They'll —

"Our gas is a chemical called methane gas. I often wonder if we could *really* blow the barn roof off." She smiles shaking her head. "American cows alone produce more greenhouse gas than 22 million cars each year! If you really want to 'go green,' don't eat us cows!

"Also, we cows are extremely over-populated. Cows are conceived through a violent, unnatural and artificial human 'aided' procedure. Too many cows are being born just so humans can eat our flesh three times a week.

"And, I mentioned earlier about the by-products that we eat. Please take this down Reporter," Tori says seriously pointing to my notebook with her chin. "Human folk should know these facts. Ready?"

I look up, pen in hand, and nod but my brain is still numb from what I've just read.

"Sixty percent of the animal agriculture cannot be used. It's called *dead stock*. This consists of parts of the animals' bodies that aren't edible, like the bones, hooves, feathers, the carcasses of animals who have died from either being too sick or who needed to be killed because of a disease outbreak on a farm, or from an accident while be transported to the slaughterhouse. Well, this ground-up animal flesh and waste is made into food for— get this — other cows. Reporter, we are herbivores — plant eaters — and the by-products in our food are forcing us into cannibalism." Tori looks at me blinking the tears back. "This sick practice is the cause of "mad cow disease" among you humans in the past, and many people have died from this disease.

What? This is mad! I'm mad! Who decides this stuff? I wipe the tears that I just realized are streaming down my cheeks. I just have to write this all down. I'll deal with my emotions later.

"Now, I'm going to get *really* disgusting. Yep," Tori nods, "I'm going to talk about our poop — someone has to! Did you read that animals, who are raised for food in this country, alone make seven million pounds of poop — every minute? That's a lot of poop. It's three times more than you humans make. Look around, Reporter, do you see any toilets here in the barn? No, and there's no right or *legal* way to get rid of all this waste, so our poop is used for fertilizer.

"What's wrong about that, you question? The combination of our methane gas and our poop, which contains nitrous oxide, has a much higher greenhouse warming potential than the carbon dioxide that worries everyone.

"With the 1.5 billion cows, our gases, and the land and the water that it takes to feed us, we are throwing the environment off into an *extremely* dangerous predicament. The future ain't what it used to be, do you know what I mean?" She looks at me but doesn't wait for an answer. "There's not much time left for this damage to be undone. I tell you, it's going to cause super-catastrophic weather events such as the places that usually get a lot of rain and snow will get hotter and drier. Droughts will occur and there will be less water for crops and drinking. Hurricanes and tornadoes will cause more destruction than ever before. Haven't you noticed that there have been more record-breaking weather events recently than any time before in history?"

Oh my goodness, she is right! There was hurricane Katrina and Super-storm Sandy and hurricane Haiyan in the Philippines, not that long ago. There was also a "once in a century" snowfall in Jerusalem recently, and this has all been in the past...few years!

"When Enzo told me this earth shattering information, I told him to stop telling me these things. The damaging numbers are so big. I just don't understand, I felt so guilty. It took a few days of comforting me and telling me that it's NOT our fault before I asked him to continue. I had to know the rest — I just had to!"

I'm writing all this down as fast as I can. I really don't believe that this information is a hundred percent accurate. How can it be true? Maybe it's just a coincidence. No wonder she's confused, upset, and feeling guilty. These are big numbers and world-changing consequences. Hey, if my gas and bowel movements threatened the planet, I'd be confused and very troubled too. I'll check the facts later. I stop writing and look up.

"Anyhoo…" Tori pauses and takes a deep breath, "the poop flows into the rivers and oceans, and the nitrous oxide sucks the oxygen out of the water. This leaves dead zones, meaning no life can survive there. We're killing the poor innocent fish too. And all this destruction for food that contributes to human folk's high blood pressure, diabetes, and heart disease," she says shaking her head. "Bon appetit," Tori adds lifting up an imaginary glass and then letting out an extremely loud…

BRRRAAAPP!

I jump. That did it! Now that one was extra loud and a real mood breaker. I'm (silently) laughing so hard, my sides hurt. I did my best! Really, I did! I explode with a loud snort! My tears are falling. I can't breathe. I'm jumping up and down with my legs crossed. Does this farm have a bathroom? And Tori is just looking at me with a confused expression. I cover my face and try to stop, but every time I try — I laugh even harder...

Then I hear a startling weird noise that stops me for a moment from laughing, and I look at Tori. She's laughing too! She's rolling on her back mooing and giggling and grunting and...

BRRRAAAPP!

And this just makes us laugh even harder!

Let's just stop for a minute and think about what has happened so far today: I hit my head and lost my voice. Then, I've chatted with an eccentric turkey, an arrogant rooster, and a hip duck, and now I'm laughing with a cow who is rolling on her back with extremely disruptive "flatulence" — AND I'm having the time of my life!

About ten minutes later, after sipping a cool drink and making a trip to the bathroom (I found a comfortable tire out back), we're calm again. This is the hardest I've ever laughed in my life — and it was with a cow!

We go back to this interview business, but this time as friends.

"THE RUNAWAY COW OF NEW YORK CITY"

"Take a flower and string it like this … yeah, you got it," Tori instructs, handing me another carnation as she speaks. "Keep going. Great work. You are a natural at this — nice job! Come on now, over here," she says, "so we can sit across from each other while we work, if you don't mind.

"Where were we? Did we start yet? First thing's first. Actually, it's the second thing but you can't say, *second thing's second*, right?" Tori mumbles, glancing at me while swatting a fly off her back with her tail.

"Anyhoo, people should be aware of how we animals — their food — travel to reach our destinations, which is sadly, in most cases, right into their big mouths! Many people just don't want to know. It's too 'scary' or 'disgusting,' they say. People live by the 'what they don't know can't hurt them' philosophy and, strangely, they choose not to know. They don't even *think* about it," Tori says as she tosses me another flower, "but these are the reasons they *should* know — it might just put a wrench in the cruelty cycle. Are you familiar with that term?" she looks up at me asking. "People might eat less meat, so there's less of a demand to *make* meat. Oh yeah, meat is made. This change would shift the demand in addition to making cleaner air and water, right? It sounds to me like you humans are brainwashed and don't, or should I say *can't*, think for yourselves? And you call yourselves intelligent?" This time she waits for my reply, but I just shake my head in disbelief. "That's just my opinion, but I'm just a cow!" She huffs, throwing up her hooves as a fistful of petals showers around us.

"Okay, moo-ving right along, my real name is Astoria, but you can call me Tori. My ear tag said 'Queen Astoria,' or was it 'Astoria, Queens?' Whatever," she mumbles shaking her head, trying to remember. "I'll start my personal story in upstate New York — that's the place I was born. My goodness, it seems like a lifetime ago. Actually, it was! I don't remember many details about my family, just deep feelings of love and snippets of memories. I had friends and my mom. Oh, my mom, I'll always miss her," she pauses, growing quiet — thoughtful. "Not a day goes by that I don't think of her." She looks away for a moment, reminiscing.

"We've heard stories about what happened to our friends when they left the farm, but we would never have guessed how tragically their lives really ended. Wait a minute," she wipes her eyes with her tail, letting out a loud, sad mooing sound. "Let me *compoooose* myself.

"The nightmare all started on the day my friends and I were shipped to the city. Funny, looking back, we weren't afraid — we were quite excited! Here we were, country cows traveling to the big city and all. We felt mature going off on our own on this new adventure. We mooed our hasty good-byes. Umm, looking back I remember that the older heifers solemnly turned their heads and walked away. We didn't have time to pack — not that we had anything. The travel arrangements weren't the best." Tori pauses for a second, "Come to think of it, they were downright crummy! Those men were rough getting us into the truck. They prodded us with the sticks if we didn't *mooove* fast enough. Without complaining, we did what they told us to do. The truck was over-crowded, and it must have been the hottest of August days. Still, our exhilaration was what kept us going. Ahhh, to be so naïve, it was a blessing! My goodness, if we only knew what was going to happen," she grimaces while shaking her head.

"Panic instantly took over the second we got there. At first, we couldn't understand what that gut wrenching sound was…" she takes a deep breath wincing, "… such a primal wail. It made me weak in the knees! We heard the resident animals screaming from their fear, misery, and pain, and every once in a while, we'd hear …" Tori gulps before continuing, 'that scream of death again.' We could even smell it. All of the other animals would be quiet for a few moments. In prayer? Too stunned to talk? I don't know I can only speak for myself." She stops for a moment, examines my string of flowers, and nods her approval before continuing.

"Anyway, the nightmare of a place we ended up in was a live slaughterhouse in Astoria, Queens, New York. Customers would come in to this place of horrors, choose the animal they wanted slaughtered, and then the poor victim would be hauled off. Someone called us, 'fresh,' but I think we were all very nice animals. I saw a few new, silly piglets, thinking it was a contest of some sort, jumping up and down squealing, 'Pick me, pick me!' They'd be picked, and then we would hear that sound again. After a while, we'd hold our breath. Instinctively, we knew what was coming. What a terrifying ordeal! The sounds and the horrifying images are still so fresh in my mind that I can't dwell on them too long without going into a fright, so bear with me if I looose it now and again.

"Miraculously, after a few days of being there, I had a flashback that saved my life—it was my light-bulb moment for me I tell you! I remember my mother saying to me, '*You* are different. *You* are going to make something of yourself.' She boasted to the other heifers that I had a clever problem-solving ability because I climbed over some boxes to get back to her one day — I don't recall the details," she says with a hoof wave. "I didn't know what she meant when I was a calf, but that thought popped into my mind at the slaughterhouse. That moment was when I decided I had to try to escape. I had to *try* for my mother. I had to try — for *me!* Sometimes, when there are no promising paths in life you have to make your own— do you understand what I mean? I had to run away the first moment I had the chance. It didn't matter where, but all I knew was those murderers had to fight if they wanted to make a hamburger out of me!

"I used to love to run when I was younger. Ahhh…" Tori smiles remembering, "It must have been my first taste of freedom. I didn't have that much room at the barn, but I had strong legs. Now, my new quest in life was to become physically powerful again. I became obsessed! Planning took up all of my mental time — it was calming, almost therapeutic. It was a distraction from the violence and death around me at the slaughterhouse. I was focused on my mission — to live. I concentrated on accomplishing this as fast as I could, which let me tell you, was hard to do because I also had to blend in with the rest of the slaughterhouse animals. What I did was this: I ate all that I could. I know..." Tori nods her head quickly as she puts a hoof up, "I know, I did feel quite selfish, but the thought of saving the future cows guiltily allowed me to actually do this. When no one was looking, I'd do my leg stretches and bends. I was getting prepared — physically, mentally, and emotionally — to get my hind outta there!

"As the days crawled by, I made plans for my moment — the turning point in my life: to live or to die. A few times I'd reconsider and pacify myself with an *it'll be alright* thought, but I knew deep down what I eventually had to do, and I hoped that I would be brave enough to do it when the time came. You know, primal fear can really motivate you to be brave.

"The big day finally came. It started out as ordinary as the day before, except late that afternoon, right before closing, a group of men came in to inspect us. I heard them talking to each other, then one of them said, 'We want that cow — the brown and white dotted animal.'

"It was *me* they wanted." She says as her breathing accelerates. "The anticipation of what was about to happen paralyzed my mind and my body. I remember standing there in shock and then I felt such a strong emotion building up. I couldn't place it. I couldn't put my hoof on it. This feeling started in my heart and in my mind simultaneously. It made me breathe funny and then all of a sudden I felt it — my eyes started to leak! I was crying! It was such a deep-rooted fear. I was afraid for my life all the way down into the pit of my stomach. I was terrified of what was about to happen to me. I wept for myself and for all the other animals that I'm sure experienced this same feeling. I cried for all the billions of future innocent beings. Why was this happening? Why was this happening to me? I didn't do anything to deserve this! I was a mess!

One man noticed me crying at this point and for a second we looked into each other's eyes. I thought we had some sort of a connection for an instant. You know, being to being. Then he heard his friends and this broke our gaze. He turned to them

164

and joked, "Look the cow's crying. Hey buddy, your porterhouse steak is getting all emotional." He laughed as he took my picture but I noticed he never looked me in the eyes again. I could feel a tear roll down my cheek right then. I shook my head and said to myself, 'Cut it out Tori and be a cow. Be a cow and make your mama proud.' My adrenaline kicked in immediately after that and it gave me the power to fight for my freedom! I had been studying the other cows the past few days — to become familiar with what to do, and also what *not* to do to cause any *commootion*. I calmed myself down and wiped my tears. My blank expression had to camouflage my brilliant escape plan. I couldn't become defiant or stand out as different than any other cow. After being prodded with the stick, I began walking slowly and steadily to 'The Room of Screams.'

"I acted as if I had stoically accepted my fate. In my daydreams I had rehearsed this scene a thousand times and, now that I had to do it, I actually felt as if I were the leading heifer in a moo-vie." Tori smiles at me, batting her eye lashes dramatically.

"I glanced at the slaughterhouse worker. For a moment I was overcome with a strange mix of emotions for him. Originally, I had such a deep-rooted hatred towards this man, yet now I only felt pity for him. He did what he had to do with that empty-headed expression on his face, day in and day out, perhaps because he simply had to. Think about it — he was just doing his job. Maybe this man wasn't educated, maybe he needed this occupation to feed his family, or maybe —for whatever reason— this was the only employment he could find. Every day he came to the slaughterhouse and murdered. Can you imagine what that can do to one's mind?" Tori looks at me blinking back tears and then shakes her head.

"Anyhoo, this was *my* moment, and I needed to concentrate on *me*. There was a door to the outside in that hallway. It was always open with the daylight shining in and, oh, the wonderful scent of independence in that city air! All I kept thinking was 'follow the light, follow *that* light.' THAT light was the path to my new life — my freedom!

Tori stops crafting, puts her hoof on my hand, and says, "So, as we approached the door, I inhaled deeply and let my instinct to live take over. Suddenly, the concept of what that man was going to do to me ignited my soul with such heated fury, I gave him one quick, hard kick —I'm not even sure where — and I ran out of that place like there was no tomorrow. Actually, I wouldn't have had a tomorrow if I didn't run! Ha Ha!" Tori shakes her head laughing as she remembers.

"My very first thought of 'I'm doing this' was such a surreal moment for me that I started to run with the speed and vigor of a thoroughbred horse — or can I say 'a thoroughbred cow?' It was all a blur, actually. I remember hearing the animal residents cheering me on as some of the slaughterhouse workers yelled after me. Other men quickly ran over to help the man who I had just kicked as he moaned, curled up on the floor. As for me, I ran and ran as fast as I could. I was so high on adrenaline that I felt as if I were flying! As the animals' voices and the sounds of the slaughterhouse men became fainter, I was instantly shocked and confused by the new loud sounds and sights of the city — they attacked my senses with the honking cars and cabs, strange smells, and I saw more people than I could ever imagine! What I had to focus on was my new sense of freedom! I then had a bizarre thought: Holy cow — I had escaped death, and I was running through New York City!

I jump up, run over to her, and give her a big hug! I've listened to her story and didn't interrupt — not that I could anyway. I cried, I laughed, and I cried again as my heart pounded from excitement and empathy. Tori made it! She made it to freedom!

Tori gives me a nuzzle with her head and continues...

"Anyhoo, I ran for my life—literally. It felt like days. Could it have been only been hours — minutes? I don't know. I was tired, sore, confused, and I needed to stop and hide. Thank goodness, I discovered a large enough alley that I was able to scoot into, so I could take a break and to collect my thoughts. At that moment, I realized my escape was all worth it — even if it was for just one hour of freedom. If the slaughterhouse workers found me and took me back at this moment, I would have thought that I lived my life. Then, I had an epiphany — it was truly a magical idea: Why should it *only* be for one hour? I wanted to live! I wanted a long life! I deserved it, and for wheat's sake, I was going to have it! Once you have a taste of freedom you are addicted to it," Tori says, nodding matter-of-factly. "I decided, whatever it took, I was going to fight with my life *for* my life. What a rush! Look, I just got cow bumps!" Tori laughs, showing me her front leg.

"I nearly jumped outta my skin as I stood there in the alley catching my breath. A vision of what I thought was an angel appeared out of nowhere. She spoke to me saying, 'Hey, you, freckle cow, what are you doing in my home?' The alley was empty, except for a few large boxes, when I got there, but now here lived a homeless woman named Cecelia, and she became my new best friend. She was peeking out from her makeshift shelter. 'You need help?" she asked. "Come here cow, to me. Don't be afraid. I will help you.'"

"I needed to trust her. Really, I had no other choice. Sirens roared as the voices got louder and louder outside the alley. I knew the men from the slaughterhouse were looking for me. I decided I *had* to trust Cecelia and believe that she would help me.

"'Come here, in the back, I hide you, 'till the commotion, he calms down, 'till the angry men go far away,' Cecelia said. 'Don't be afraid, pretty cow. I am a good woman for you.' I followed her and she gave me some water.

"As we heard the angry voices of the slaughterhouse men coming closer, Cecelia covered me with a large blanket and whispered, 'Do not you move, cow!' Cecelia lived humbly. You might even call it a 'dirt poor' life, but there was nothing timid about her strength and determination to defend me. When we heard a man shout, 'Maybe that crazy beast of a cow is in here.' HA- HA! My protector ran

over to them swinging a bat! The language on her —
I won't repeat it — but take my word, it was shocking!

"After they left, she saw how upset and shaken
I still was, and she sang softly into my ear. I didn't
understand the words, but her song relaxed me a bit.
Her gentle touch and her kindness — how could I
have lived my life without ever feeling this? Actually,
this was the first day I realized I *had* feelings, and do
you know what? I kinda liked it," Tori says with a
sweet smile on her face. "Maybe I had these feelings
with my Mom, but I was too young to remember. It
seemed like a lifetime ago that I knew her." She
stops and lets out a long sigh. "It was a heartbreaking, bittersweet moment for me because I
missed her so very much. I hoped she was okay and
wasn't worrying about me. I then realized that I had
to learn to harden my heart against my yearning for
her in order to go on with my new life. She would
have been filled with pride if she knew what I
accomplished," Tori nods smiling.

"I just experienced the most exciting, luckiest,
best, yet scariest day of my life — all rolled into a few
hours — but I was too emotionally and physically
drained to even think about it. Cecelia sensed my
exhaustion and said, 'You rest now freckle cow. I am
here for you.'

"I settled on her lap feeling as if I were emotionally wrapped in a security blanket. I had surrendered to a comforting embrace of sleep as I floated off to paradise and dreamt that I was on a heavenly farm, the atmosphere filled with kindness. It was a farm without any fear. All the animals were happy. I could stroll in the pastures of real grass never having to look over my shoulder in fear. I even felt it tickling my hooves," she says smiling. "I must have had too much fresh air that day — what a dream! It was the most peaceful sleep I enjoyed in my whole life — *my life!* I now felt that I had a future. I never had that sensation before. Although this feeling was foreign to me, it had given me strength. I still feel giddy with excitement thinking back. Ohhhh, look, my cow bumps are back again!" She shouts, shoving her big front leg in my face.

"The next morning, I woke up with Cecelia combing my hair. 'Freckles,' she said twisting her head to the side as she read my ripped ear-tag, 'You have name of 'Tori,'' she said smiling. She then christened me with my first New York City meal — pretzels from a vendor! I later learned that the tag read 'Astoria, Queens,' but only 'tori' was legible.

"She had gone out that first night, right after I had fallen to sleep, to tell her homeless friends and

171

the street vendors about me. She asked them for help in protecting and hiding me. Word spread fast on the streets, and with their aid, I was able to live without fear — so I thought. I never made plans past my escape. What was I thinking? My only thought was to survive! What nice, friendly people they were to help me! They fed me the freshest apples, handfuls of green grass from Central Park — food never tasted so delicious! I thought, I could get used to this living. I could get used to living — period!

"Cecelia had a heavy European accent, so it was sometimes difficult for me to understand her. Nevertheless, she was motherly to me and treated me as if I were her own daughter. I was apprehensive during my first few days of freedom but quickly comfortable in the security of my new home in the alley and with my new protector. Such an exciting way to live, I thought. Then after the initial thrill wore off, reality set in; I was beginning to become very despondent with my situation. I realistically couldn't live *here* forever.

"Cecelia caught me crying one night. I didn't know what to do or how to feel. I was becoming too dependent on her. She made me feel protected and loved. I decided at that point that my brilliant plan might not have been too brilliant after all. I didn't want to overstay my welcome. I knew I had to eventually leave. As she stroked my head to comfort me, she said that night, 'You are a brave young cow, full of the fight in you. Do not let your past predict how you should live the tomorrows of your life. Let your new wisdom of freedom show to you, your future. You must go, be free, and tell the others. Warn them, the other animals, and help them. You have nothing to lose, only this chance in your life to live. You cannot stay here forever, but you know I and all your friends will help you.'

"Her love and confidence in me encouraged me to develop ways to renew my weakening spirit. In a few days, her friends had donated clothes and wigs for me to wear so I wouldn't be recognized as what the newspapers called me: '*The Runaway Cow of New York City*.' I learned to trust others, maybe too much. I don't know, but I was having the time of my life. It's ironic that I started to have my best days right after it was supposed to end. Weird, huh?"

No? Yes? I don't want to nod or shake too much and possibly distract her from continuing her story, so I just smile. I'm so proud of her! What a brave cow she is!

"The first time I left the alley, Cecelia dressed me up very stylish. I wore a long braided blond wig, with a pretty, pink bandana behind my ears. One nice Russian street vendor donated sunglasses to complete my ensemble.

"Oh! I still have them here!" Tori shouts, rummaging through her box of *STUFF* again, and pulls out a huge pair of *Ray-Barn* sunglasses. She looks at them, remembering her adventures, and then puts them on smiling. "Cecelia showed me my reflection in a small mirror that she owned. It was actually the first time I had ever seen myself, and to be honest with you," Tori says oozing with confidence, "I was — I AM — quite beauu-ti-ful!

"I walked around the block, hesitantly at first, taking just a few steps at a time and cautiously looking around. Do you know what?" she recalls with a chuckle, "I fit right in! I looked like a tourist, which enabled me to do some sightseeing throughout Manhattan!

"The street vendors still gave me food. Others told me if my tail was showing or if I was acting too *cowish*. These friendly people were all so incredibly helpful.

"I enjoyed my adventures for a few days. I traveled to the Statue of Liberty on the ferryboat. A vendor gave me a green Statue of Liberty foam crown to wear," Tori says, smiling as she dumps the rest of her treasures from her box onto the table. She searches for a few minutes, shrugs her shoulders, and with one sweep of her hoof pushes all her things back into the box.

"The people didn't recognize me, but all of the animals did. The curious looks I got from the park's snickering squirrels. Ha Ha! And the double takes I got from the rats. A few carriage horses said, 'You go girl,' while I strolled through the park munching on a bag of peanuts. I felt so lucky. I had considered going to the zoo, but I thought it was best that I didn't.

"One Sunday, Cecelia applied fancy makeup and false eye lashes on me. I wore another blond, curly wig – I do prefer to be a blond," Tori adds, casually flipping imaginary hair over her shoulder. "Cecelia told me that she was going to doll me up pretty. 'I take you to see the houses of the rich,' she said, and then we went strolling on *Madison Ave.* What a life!

"Just then it happened. I was recognized! There was confusion, noise, the sound of the sirens, and the sound of Cecelia screaming before a cop shot me with a tranquilizer gun. I blacked out. It all happened so fast that I didn't have a chance to think — or to panic.

"When I woke up, I was back at the slaughterhouse. Instantaneously, I felt a familiar, dreadful fear down to my soul, but with all of the recognition I received being on national TV as 'The Cow Who Ran Through the New York City Streets,' I didn't have to stay long and —they treated me kinda nice too."

"I was told that the slaughterhouse received hundreds of calls to release me. My story was in the *Associated Press*, *The New York Times*, and *The New York Daily News*. Farmer Harry heard about me and immediately came to my rescue. My hero! Eventually, the slaughterhouse closed and was fined hundreds of dollars because of the filthy and horrendous conditions and inhumane treatment of the animals. Unfortunately, the animals were transported to another slaughterhouse. On a happier note, one hundred and fifty chickens were freed. YIPPEE for them!

"Farmer Harry took me to my new home at Animal Haven. I must say that the New York City skyline looked very beauu-ti-ful as I was leaving! As the trailer pulled up to the farm, I had a content feeling of belonging, and I knew I was safe. Everyone cheered for me as I jumped out! Strange ..." Tori says to me with a puzzled expression. "It was *déjà moo* all over again; I felt it immediately. *This* was the farm that I dreamt about; *this* was the farm where the chickens happily 'clucked;' pigs 'squealed' with delight; goats 'naaaed' with enthusiasm; and the cows 'mooed' their welcomes. *This* is what animals should sound like. Astoria, Queens #042383 had finally arrived. This..." Tori stands up and bows, "was my Hollywood ending. I was home!"

I leap up again and give her a well-deserved round of applause. She just stares at me. Maybe she doesn't understand the "hand clapping" ritual. Maybe she thinks I have flies bothering me. I sit back down with a big smile on my face. What a story! What an amazing cow!

"I received immediate medical attention and, understandably, I needed counseling. I got Farmer Harry's version of a 'hoof up' for a good health report in just a few days. That's when I met my two gal pals, Charlene and Cheyenne, at therapy. We got to chatting, and holy cow was I surprised when I found out how much I had in common with these ladies, my 'soul sistas.'

MOO-VING TALES

"Cows like to wear the leis *loooose;* make them a little longer, if you don't mind. You're doing a fantastic job, Reporter." Tori smiles at me while nodding her approval.

"Let me tell you a little about my girls before I walk you to the pigs' pen. Charlene, we call her Charlee, you might have heard about her. Her real name is Charlene Moo-ken, but she's infamously known as 'Cincinnati Freedom.' Google her when you get home. She was on TV too. Her tale began after she leapt over a six-foot fence escaping from a slaughterhouse in Ohio. The slaughterhouse workers searched eleven days before they found her. HA!" Tori chuckles with a big smile. "Whatta girl!

"When the workers finally did catch her, they couldn't send her back to the slaughterhouse because, as news reports said, *'Now the people of Cincinnati know where their pot roast comes from.'* Many people called in to house her: zoos, circuses, ordinary people who just wanted her for their backyard. However, the person who was concerned for her protection the most was the famous painter Peter Max, who is a vegan.

"Peter Max offered paintings worth — I don't remember off hoof, but they were worth a lot of money, in exchange for her freedom to live here at Animal Haven. That lucky heifer even has the key to the city from the mayor, Mr. Luken. She wears it around her neck on special events and holidays. She didn't like the media attention at all back then. She's still not too friendly with people. I tell you though, visitors change after meeting her and reading her story. I suppose they realize they can help save farm animals by becoming vegans or at least vegetarians.

Vegans and Vegetarians — isn't that the same thing? And, as if reading my mind, Tori says:

"Now the difference between a vegan and a vegetarian is that vegans, in addition to not eating meat like a vegetarian, don't eat fish or anything *derived* from any living creature, such as milk, eggs, and honey. In fact, they also don't wear any items *made* from animals, such as leather shoes or jackets, or wool. And please," Tori growls, shaking her fisted hoof in the air, "don't get me started with the selfish *moo-rons* who think they look beau-ti-ful in fur coats!"

Besides all of the meat, milk, and ice cream I've eaten, I now have to re-think my wool sweaters and

179

my down comforters, I've also worn many leather shoes and belts. I recently spent a lot of money for a "nice" leather jacket. What was I thinking? What wasn't I thinking? I want to say "thank you," but does that justify all that they've given us? But...these things weren't given, they were stolen away. As well as my eating habits, I also have to consider my clothing choices. I will change, there is no question about it — these are now my animal friends!

"It's a commitment to live a compassionate lifestyle," Tori says seriously. "You'd be surprised. It can be done—and it's healthier, too."

I continue to write my notes as I nod my head – I agree. I'm ashamed. There's so much I don't know, and there's so much that I've taken for granted all these years.

"Remember many years ago when people thought smoking was actually healthy for you?" she asks, shaking her head. "Doctors even promoted it to *'relieve stress,'* they would say. Now it's known to cause cancer, birth defects, and other diseases. It's even *taboooo* to smoke in restaurants or public buildings nowadays. I hope that eating animal flesh will soon be the new controversy. I can see it now my friend; they'll have warning labels on meat: 'Eat this meat at your own risk. It causes heart disease,

180

diabetes, high blood pressure, high cholesterol, stroke, and eventually — death.' Or..." Tori laughs slapping her knee, "I'd love to see a picture of a cow with 'RIP Matthew, you were a good bull,' written on it and left with the packaged meat at the supermarkets. HaHa! That might wake some people up to *our* reality.

"Anyhoo, it's 'trendy' nowadays to be a vegetarian, but it's only a matter of time until human folk will realize that people who do not eat meat, or even less meat, are healthier, have less body fat, and have a longer lifespan than those who do. You'll see, mark my words.

"Did ya know that meat has no fiber? Fiber is the roughage that lowers cholesterol and burns calories. It's only found in plant-based food."

Okay...I am trying to understand. But what about the protein?!

"It's funny, because the *first* thing people always ask when someone says that they are vegetarian is: 'What about the protein?'" Tori looks at me somehow knowing my thoughts again. "'You're not getting enough protein if you don't eat meat,' people say, quickly assuming and then dismissing any thought that they could possible be wrong. All of a sudden, everyone thinks that they're a dietary expert! Do they worry about the majority of the people who are getting *too much* protein? Never!

"There are a variety of nuts, whole grains, soy products, vegetable protein burgers, and other meat-alternative foods. Broccoli has the same amount of protein, if not more, than cow flesh — without the fat! Have you checked the large selection at most neighborhood supermarkets lately? Have you seen all of the new 'health food' stores opening? Yet, these same 'experts' aren't concerned that a diet, that is too high in protein, is linked to kidney disease, osteoporosis; and cancers of the colon, breast, prostate, and pancreas. There is so much information out there! I want to tell them, 'Come on people. You have a computer, you have a brain, AND you even have fingers. Look it up!'"

I'm feeling ignorant right now. Looking back, I should have realized it's some kind of an agricultural scam. Why haven't I ever researched my own food choices? Why did I blindly trust doctors to tell me what to eat? Did the United States Department of Agriculture really invent the food pyramid to guide us?

"Enzo explained to me that there are two ways human folk are fooled. One way is that human folk believe what *isn't* true. The other way is that they refuse to believe what *is* true."

I nod, agreeing with Tori. This is exactly how it is!

"Then you get the sarcastic ones that ask, 'Now, what about those poor carrots? Aren't they alive? Don't they have feelin's too?' Ohhhhhh please!" Tori emphasizes dramatically with an eye roll. "I have no comments for those *moo-rons*!"

"And that's not all. Did you know that due to these hand-me-down habits of the parents, kids in America today have levels of obesity and chronic illness never before seen in human history? Enzo told me that he was reading an article by John Robbins, who wrote *'The Food Revolution.'* When these children become young adults, they will likely develop a range of illnesses including heart disease. One in three children will develop type 2 diabetes.

"What's really crazy, listen to this, food manufacturers spend roughly $10 *billion* dollars every year *just* to advertise junk food to children. Aren't there poor people throughout the world that could use that money for a good meal or two?"

I look up from writing in my notebook. What?! Did she just say: "$10 billion, with a "B," *just* to advertise nutritional deficient food and encourage poor eating habits to children? Isn't there a recession going on? What about the national deficit? Is this a conspiracy? Are terrorists involved? Does our government know? Do they allow this? WHY?

I sit there stunned, deep in thought while doodling question marks all over my page of notes. I have a lot of research to do when I get home.

"On one hoof I didn't think this was right, but on the other hoof I wouldn't doubt it. I asked Enzo if this was moral and legal, but apparently, it is. Strange world we live in, huh? I guess it's all about the moo-la," she says as she hits her front hooves together. "Besides eating meat, especially from sick or dying animals, unsuspecting children are overeating junk food that contains high amounts of sugar, saturated fat, cholesterol, chemicals, sodium and ...GMO foods — Ha! — there's an interesting topic alone! But, any-hoo, I suppose what human child wouldn't want a *Happy Meal,* consisting of cleverly advertised junk food, and a sugary soda, and then even get a toy with it? Such a shame," Tori says shaking her head. "It's a psychological ploy to make money at the expense of innocent kids! Think about it, these unhealthy children are hooked on this 'food,' crave it, and before you know it, you have a new generation of sick people struggling with obesity and illnesses.

This generation of children could be the first who don't outlive their parents. Is that healthy progress?"

Tori is right! She's very intelligent. All the animals at Animal Haven know so much—actually more than most people do. Too bad we all can't hear their stories and their voices. Ohhhh....now I get it! I can be their voice! But I can't speak now. How am I...? Umm, I don't understand how this is going to... Just keep writing — write it all down. I'll get to it when I get my voice back.

"My other pal Cheyenne, received a Presidential Medal of Freedom. You might have heard about her famous, 'I am Honored and Humbled' speech?'"

I shrug my shoulders.

"Well, Cheyenne was a fugitive for over six months after escaping from the auction. She roamed around the New England countryside and was brave enough to cross over rivers and highways. Eventually she befriended her Ma and Pa, who just happen to be friends of Farmer Harry. She would visit them at their house for dinner every night. She left Ma and Pa C's house kicking up her heels and skipping all the way back to her secret home. She was so happy just to have friends again.

"One day she decided she had had enough living by herself. Independent living is not so easy when you are all alone, but I guess that's what independent living is all about, huh?" Tori says, fumbling with her thoughts, then continues. "Anyhoo…one night she walked into their barn and into their hearts. They had a long talk with her about Animal Haven. It sounded too good to be true, she thought, but she trusted Ma and Pa. The next day Farmer Harry came and took her to her new home. It's truly amazing that everyone says that as soon as you get here, you feel at home. You know you belong."

Uh-huh, it's true. I do feel quite comfortable here, but belong…I don't know.

"Well, look who it is — it's Joey! He's my brother from a different ma-tha — and fa-tha, too. No, wait," Tori pauses, thinking for a moment. "I mean, he's also from New York — like me! We are not *really* related, for wheat's sake. He's a goat and I'm a cow!

"How are you doing, Joey?!"

"Tori, look at you, as beautiful as ever! I'm fine, but I'm in a hurry. I'll see you tomorrow. Behave now! Love to the girls!"

"Take it easy, Joey!" Torí says as she waves her tail.

Look at this, a talking goat! Not like this has been the strangest thing that I've seen all day. How cute is he? A bit of a tough guy. He's even wearing a little gold hoop earring.

"Joey, he's a good goat. He loves to joke around, play — see how big he is? He's a Boer goat — was only six months old when they found him wandering around Brooklyn, N.Y., his ear still tagged for slaughter. He wears an earring now to cover it. Either he's very private or he doesn't remember much, other than he lived at a religious butcher — Kosher or a Halal — he's not sure. Supposed to mean 'humane slaughter,' but isn't that a...what is the word? 'Ox-is-moron?' It's like a 'good' kick in the behind. What's humane about it? Anyhoo, Kosher and Halal have similarities and differences, but the end result is the same - a sharp knife, a prayer, and a dinner for the family."

THOSE AMAZING PIGS

"Now we have to get you to those pigs," Tori says while holding up the last lei admiring it. "I hope they aren't waiting for you. Let me just tidy up a bit while I tell you a few facts about pigs, then we'll be on our way."

Tori drags her craft box out from under the table. She's very meticulous in organizing her materials. The ribbons curled tightly, the paints are stored from light to dark, and she has little baggies of buttons, silk flowers, and assorted do-dads. I try to help, but she stops me with her hoof.

"First of all, pigs are highly gifted beings. They love music, and I've heard them discussing the meaning of their dreams with each other. In fact, they are so intelligent that they are often compared with a three or four-year-old human child. Most of them, no offense, are much nicer than human children!" Tori says, cautiously waiting for my reaction.

Get out of here! Pigs are as smart as pre-schoolers? I'm surprised to hear that!

"Most people have the wrong impression of pigs. They believe that pigs are very dirty animals —

188

that's totally false! HaHa! Many of the pigs here at Animal Haven volunteer for the cleanup committee because they don't think any of us can do a good enough job.

"It makes me sick to think that 105 million of these pleasant, clean, intellectual, sociable, musically-inclined, loving animals are slaughtered each year..." she hesitates, "...to become your baked ham, pulled pork, bacon, pork chop, or loin of pork dinner. This just doesn't make any sense to me," she grunts. "And I know for a fact that those pigs have no ribs to spare!

"Those cute little piglets are nursed for only two to three weeks and then are snatched from their moms. They are housed in overcrowded crates until they're about six months old or 250 pounds — whichever comes first. Moms put up a huge fight when they take their babies away, and do you know why? BECAUSE THEY LOVE THEM — that's why!"

Tori yells while banging her hoof on the table. A ball of yarn flies off the table and unravels as it rolls across the barn. I jump up, running after it. She waits for me to sit before she continues.

"We animals love our babies. It's frightening how misunderstood we all are! A sow, a mother pig, would normally enjoy hanging out with other mom pigs, just as humans do, at the playgrounds and such. They'll chat about their boars, their husbands, and what they are making for dinner. They'll discuss piglet care, and I'm sure also do their share of gossiping," Tori adds with a smile. "At dirty factory farms, the sows are confined in undersized gestation crates that are only two feet wide." She shows me the size by measuring with her hooves. "The crates are so small that the sows can't turn around or take more than one step forward or backward. Because of the amount of time and the brutality of this confinement, these pigs suffer both physically and mentally. Their experience is among the worst tortures of all factory-farmed animals. They'll rub themselves raw against the bars or gnaw on the bars because of the lack of mental stimulation, and of course, the sores go untreated. After the trauma of losing their babies, the moms are re-impregnated. In other words they are ... *violated* with machinery and repeatedly go through this trauma repeatedly... which is a lot because the moms can give birth twice a year! They live this kind of life until they can no longer reproduce and are considered useless — then they are then sent off to the ...slaughterhouse."

"Ribs," I think. Baby back ribs. Baby's BACK ribs... are, BABIES...ribs! I cover my mouth as I

have a flashback. I'm about 13 years old and it's
Sunday afternoon dinner. My brothers were out, and
my dad was working, so it was just my mom and me.
It was a cozy, rainy afternoon, and we were enjoying
each other's company while watching *The African
Queen*, a movie that I had never seen before. We
were sitting in the kitchen watching TV and nibbling
on… a pan full of ribs! We were eating baby pigs!

I run out of the barn, and I throw up at the side
of the road with tears in my eyes. Babies!! I'm sure
that I never thought of piglets on that memorable
day. I start throwing up again. Tori comes over giving
me a "that's-okay-you-didn't-know" look. How many
times can I say I'm sorry? We walk back into the
barn. I don't know if I want to hear anymore. I'm tired.
My head still hurts. I still can't speak. Then I notice
that Tori is staring at me. She has a compassionate
look in her eye. I know that she understands how I
feel. I've never realized how all animals are just like
— us.

I then think about my puppy, Benjamin Franklin,
he's my baby boy, I would never let anything happen
to him. Imagine in other countries…I gasp and stop
myself from finishing this thought. Then I remember
the cover of the booklet that pamphlet-guy from the

train shoved in my face: "Why eat one but not the other?"

What about all the people who are against cruelty to animals? They get furious, as they should, for a poorly treated dog or cat. They post all kinds of articles about saving the dolphins and cutesy kittens along with information about adopting sheltered dogs, and then some of them go home and grill a steak or have some chicken's wings. I don't understand!

Tori pauses to make sure I'm okay and then continues. "On a lighter note, do you know how long pigs are pregnant for? The girls and I were just talking about this last week. 114 days is a pig's gestation time." Tori looks at me enthusiastically, but I just shrug. "'So what,' you think! That's 3 months, 3 weeks and 3 days! 3, 3, 3! Do you know how magical that is? I've been interested in numbers ever since living in New York City and finding my way on those numbered streets. These are just my thoughts: there are three divisions of time: past, present and future," she says as she ticks off on her toes. "There are three states that define life: animal, vegetable, mineral. There are three persons in grammar: me, myself and I; humans have three abilities: thought, word, and deed. Then, there's faith, hope, and love;

the religious trinity and the…!" Tori's smile begins to fade because I'm not sharing her excitement.

"Anyhoo, not for nothing, it made a good conversation on a rainy day. The goats even got involved in this discussion.

"So back to the pigs, if that's okay with you?"

I nod, yes. What am I going to say, "no?" A good reporter reports, and that's what I'm here to do. Let me just make sure my face is clean of vomit first.

"I do want to share some good news," Tori says, smiling. "Many animal activists are now fighting against this brutal confinement practice right now, even if it's just to make the moms a little more comfortable with bigger crates. It's up to the governor in each state to change these laws. Please reporter, write to your congressional representative when you get home. All in all, it's a step in the right direction.

"One more thing about the factory piglets, please write this down," she hesitates, but I nod indicating that I'm ready. "The little piggies have their tails cut off; their ears are also cut so they can be identified. Of course this is all done without any anesthesia," she winces. "Sad thing is that if you gave a three-week-old pig a name, like we do here at Animal Haven, they are smart enough to learn it and will answer you when called. In addition, piglets who are only a few hours old will leave their nest to go to the bathroom on their own. In other words, they potty train themselves when they are born. It takes human children years to learn this, right?" she asks with a smug expression. "Personally, besides being nicer, I believe they're smarter than human children too!"

That's not nice! I give Tori a mock insulted face. She might be right though, but I see she's teasing me. She's kinda cute with that silly grin on her face.

"Pigs form close bonds with each other and with other animals too. They love to cuddle with their close friends while they're resting. If you give a pig a belly-rub, you'll have a friend for life! We have some fantastic pigs living here at Animal Haven."

THE NEWLYWEDS

SQUEAK!

"Yoohoo, Tori, where *are* you?!"

"WHAT a coincidence!" Tori gasps, "Here *are* the pigs!! You can't make this stuff up! It's Carole and Rudy Pig — our newlyweds!

"We were just on our way to visit you."

LOOK— PIGS!

As if on cue, two huge pigs walk into the barn. I'm beside myself with excitement; I've always wanted to meet a pig! Without thinking, I leap up, run over, and give one a hug. They are enormous but appear to be friendly. They both smile at me, nodding hesitantly. The female, the one I'm hugging, is the stereotypical quintessential feminine pig, (What?! Is there such a concept?) complete with a bonnet, long eyelashes, curly hair, and a graceful demeanor.

"Hi Tori! Who's this affectionate one here?" Carole asks.

"It's our visitor, Reporter. She's writing a story about us. I was a bit skeptical of her at first, but she's okay for a human folk. Reporter has been through a lot today," Tori says sympathetically. "She lost her voice — can't seem to find it anywhere — and she has been experiencing a lifetime of guilt this morning while trying to grasp our reality."

"Understandable," Carole sighs. "Guilt - there's a trip I don't see enough people going on these days. She does need a hug then."

Carole looks at me sweetly, and then nuzzles my chin. She is plump, yet attractive. I look into her eyes, suddenly feeling as if we've met before. How could I know her? It can't be, I don't know any pigs. Her eyes look so … human, familiar, and full of emotion with a strange sense of understanding. She reminds me of someone I once knew. But who? Suddenly, a bizarre thought of friendship, familiarity, and — bacon collide together. I struggle for breath and pull away, I guess too suddenly. She looks at me alarmed. How can I get all that from looking into a pig's eyes? Then I remember what Romeo told me earlier: I would fall in love with a pig if I looked into their eyes.

"What are you two doing here?" Tori asks.

"Tori, Carole and I were strolling over to the pond for a cooling mud bath. Carole then suggested that we stop by for a visit to see if you needed any help with last-minute fixings for the feast," Rudy replies. "How's everything going here?"

"Everything is under control," Tori answers waving her hoof, "but I won't say no to help. I could use someone to clean the dance area a little." Tori turns to me whispering, "Watch how excited they get because I said the word 'clean.'"

"We'd LOVE to help clean," they both squeal delightfully.

Tori says, "I was just telling Reporter how great pigs are! She is going to write a story about our home here."

Carole and Rudy both smile at me while nodding their heads in approval.

"As I said, she's safe, even rather pleasant, for a human folk," she says admirably in my direction. "Why don't you both tell her your love story? I need to see how many flowers I have left. They're in the back of the barn."

"Well, okay. Carole is a bit shy, but I love talking about how we met," says Rudy, putting his front leg around Carole to pull her closer. Carole seems not to be able to resist Rudy with his knowing smile, cute flat nose and his gray eyes that seem to twinkle whenever he speaks to her.

"Oh honey, I'm not shy, I'm just a little reserved about sharing how much I love you. I *am* a private pig."

197

"I love you too, my tootsie-wootsie." Rudy coos as they give each other a snout rub. "We were childhood sweethearts," he says affectionately without breaking his gaze from Carole. "We were born just a few crates away. Our moms were best friends."

"How I do miss my Mama, Rudy! And your mama, Auntie Annie, was a real sweet sow, very protective of her piglets and her friends' babies, too. They did the best they could in those inhumane, tiny gestation crates that they were stuck in – never complained in front of us. We couldn't even nurse in the same crate she was in – much too small." She shakes her head turning to Rudy, "Enzo said that people are fighting to phase out those torturous crates that are banned in many European nations. But our mamas loved us, they did!"

"Our moms used to whisper words of encouragement to us at night to calm us down while putting us to sleep," he says looking past me with a hint of melancholy in his voice. "They'd say: 'Always walk with your head up and follow the tail in front of you.'" Rudy grimaces, realizing his mistake. He cautiously glances at Carole to see if she heard him. "They knew we would be taken from them soon."

"TAILS! Look at our stubby ...!" Carole cries, unable to finish the sentence. Rudy immediately puts his front leg around her again.

I quickly glance at her tail. It is a bit short and choppy — like a bad haircut.

"Sweet baby-mud-cakes, it's okay! I am so sorry for mentioning the word 'tail.' You have the most beautiful... tail..." he hesitates, "I've ever seen!" Rudy says, trying to console her. He looks at me to finish his conversation. "You see, since we were leaving our mamas at three weeks old, instead of the normal 13 weeks, we now have a lifelong craving to gnaw. At the overcrowded factory farm, because of boredom, anxiety, and aggravation, we would bite each other's tails. Hey, you would too," he adds.

I put my hands up indicating that I don't know anything about tails — but I do sympathize with them.

He continues, "So, without any anesthesia, and with a pair of dull pliers, they cut and ripped off our tails to stubs. They say it's done *humanely* but... "

I cover my face in horror, as I get weak in the knees. I can only imagine how painful that was for them.

"...this makes our tails super sensitive — so much so, that if another pig tries to chew on it, it's a reflex to jump away. Ohhhhh and on castration day..." Rudy squeals, trailing off with a shudder.

"Please, honey, no, no, nooo, don't..." Now it's Carole's turn to comfort Rudy. "You know you'll be up all night tossing and turning."

The passion between these two is incredible. Rudy begins to relax as Carole rubs his head.

She turns to me and explains, "The umbrella for these so-called 'humane' treatments cover so many brutal practices besides tail-docking and ... castration," she adds in a barely audible whisper. She takes a deep breath and continues, "such as thumping."

I shrug my shoulders and shake my head, I've never heard of that.

"Thumping is when the smallest piglet of a litter, a runt, is violently thrown against the wall to kill them. Enzo told me he read that it's not economically wise to keep this little innocent being. I remember my tiny brother being taken away from us." She wipes her fresh tears with the back of her hoof. "Even this is considered 'humane' under federal standards — supposedly this is also pain free."

Carole sits there for a few moments, trying to calm herself with deep, steady breaths. She then wiggles up a little taller, puts on a forced cheerful face and says, "Okay now, I'll tell the rest of *our* happier story!" She waits for a second, smiling. "Our day finally came ... do you think our moms knew that we were leaving that day?" Carole turns to Rudy, but he's still in a trance from his head being rubbed and doesn't reply. "I remember bolting out of my sleep when I heard the awful sound of chains clanking. I hated that noise, still do! After being grabbed and thrown into that crowded truck, we were on our way to the finishing farm or the fattening farm before ... before we were going to be slaughtered. We tried to stay together, but at one point I ... I couldn't find you!" Carole cries out as they hold each other remembering.

AWWW. These two really do love each other!

Rudy takes Carole's face with both his hooves. He looks at her and says, "Carole, stop. I did find you, remember? It's okay, my honey-bee. Shhhh. We pushed our way to the back of the truck. I tried comforting you by telling you the piggy-tale story my mama had once told me. It was a story about a little pig who did *not* follow the tail in front of him, instead he followed his heart, and his dreams. You looked up at me," he says lovingly to Carole. "I can still recall that pleading and excited look in your eyes, as you said —"

"I said, 'Rudy, THIS is what we have to do, together.'" Carole shouts, taking over this part of the story. "You were confused, and so I explained that when the truck slowed down, we'd crawl to the top of the other pigs, hold hooves, close our eyes, and jump! It was a dangerous plan, but we had to do something and this sounded like the best thing at the time. What did we have to lose? We had each other!"

"And that's what we did!" they both squeal in unison with silly grins on their faces.

"Carole, you are so romantic, my dear." Rudy squeezes her into his arms and looks at her with such a depth of feelings in his eyes. She returns his loving gaze as he continues.

"The truck stopped at a railroad crossing," Rudy explains. "We excused ourselves as we climbed up over the pigs. They all looked at us as if we were crazy. They said their 'good-byes' and their 'good lucks,' and then we did it — we jumped! Ha-ha! We took our leap of faith, or our 'leap of love' as we call it now. I think we were both pretty surprised how easy it was when we landed." He laughs as they both nod at each other.

"It was a cloudy day..." Carole smiles nostalgically. "It's funny how you remember the minor details. As soon as we jumped out, the sun started to shine. Oh, what a deliciously warm glow it was welcoming us to our new chance at life. We were both giddy with excitement, hurtling towards our future together. I can still hear you, my wild boar, you couldn't stop snorting! You had tears coming out of your eyes as you giggled and grunted! Our lives rolled out ahead of us like one of those endless rolls of white drawing paper. It was up to us now to design our future together. We ran and ran until we couldn't run anymore. I must have twisted my ankle. We weren't used to running so far," Carole says looking at me. "We weren't used to running at all, come to think of it. We then found a nice place — our first home together on our own!" She makes a little snort, as if recalling those first precious moments. "Oh, such fun! Oh, Rudy, we thought we were safe. We thought this was how our new life was going to be. We had no plans for the future. I suppose, in hindsight, that the best preparedness in our situation was not being prepared at all," she says with a shrug. "We lived from day to day. It wasn't easy. After a few weeks of not eating right and not having enough water and with my ankle still giving me trouble, I guess we got careless. We let our guard down, and someone found us. Thank goodness she was a sweet lady."

"She *was* a very kind lady," Rudy nods in agreement. "She had compassion in her eyes, and her ethereal mannerisms comforted us into trusting her right away. I think at that point in our adventure we had to believe in someone. She took us to her home, put some *oinkment* on your leg, and promised that she would find a nice, safe place for us.

"It was fortunate that a friend of hers told her *not* to send us to that petting zoo. It sounded like a nice place. I know how you were excited to be around children, but do you know what they do to those cute, little animals at the end of the season?" Rudy directs his question towards me, and then pauses.

"Rudy, no – don't say it!"

"Sweetie, let me tell the story. People need to know, and she *is* a reporter. I'm sure she is used to hearing all sorts of hardships." He turns in my direction to explain, "Those precious baby animals, that the children adore all summer, are sent to the slaughterhouse at the end of the season!"

I'm horrified! I put both hands on my head as I remember that I used to love going to those petting farms. Is this really what happens to them?! I once befriended a little black goat named Alma who was rescued from a highway in Jersey City. I told her my secrets and pretended that she could understand me. Actually, I was sure that she did because she winked at me when I made her promise not to tell anyone. I was so excited to visit her at the petting zoo the following year, but she wasn't there. I ran around to all the fenced in areas calling her name. To calm me down my mom finally had to ask one of the workers where Alma was. He just shrugged his shoulders because he didn't know what we were talking about. My heart was broken. My mom told me that she moved to another farm, far away. She convinced me that Alma made new friends and even had a family of her own. That made me feel a little better but I never forgot her. Oh, my little friend, my Alma, I'm sad to imagine what really happened to her.

Another memory comes back to me: We would pet the animals at the petting zoo and learn how they live, then, only 20 feet away in the picnic area, we would sit down and have a hamburger or hot-dog lunch. I never ever thought about the irony of this situation. What a strange concept — that people don't connect their food that they are eating with live animals that they were just petting. Huh!

I run over and give them each another hug. I love these pigs! I can't change what I've done in the past, but I'm here to learn and change what I do in the future, and maybe I can also help others to change.

"To make a long story short," Carole continues when she sees me looking at her again, "the nice lady found out about Animal Haven and drove us here in her convertible." She turns to Rudy asking, "Remember dear, she gave me her kerchief so my hair wouldn't mess? Oh such fun!"

"Yes, stunning! You looked like my perfect sow!" Rudy answers.

"And that's our story," Carole says. "We lived —"

"Happily ever after," Rudy finishes for her, giving Carole a snout rub with tender kisses.

"Oh, Rudy, *stop!*" Carole blushes, noticing Tori nearby. "I didn't see you come back. Those leis look absolutely beautiful! The whole barn looks magnificent. You outdid yourself again."

GOOD GRIEF

"Rudy, would you be a sweetheart? I need your help to MOO-ve a big crate," Tori asks, already walking to the back of the barn before he answers. "It's blocking the back exit of the barn…fire hazard. I need someone strong."

"Of course, Tori, anything you need me to do. I'm at your service," Rudy answers with a big smile and then turns to Carole. "My lovey-dovey, will you be alright without me?"

"Oh Rudy, go and take your time. Reporter is here with me. She and I need some girl time anyway." Carole nudges me with her hefty front leg, smiling. "There're a few things I need to discuss with her. Girl talk," she adds, crinkling up her nose. Rudy playfully mouths *I love you* before he turns away.

Uh-oh! Did I do something wrong? Is she insulted because I pulled away from her hug before? I won't explain my reasoning to her; I might hurt her feelings. Ha! I couldn't if I wanted to. Whew, I'm in the clear. I'm anxious to know why she needs to speak with me. I look over as Tori and Rudy shift the boxes around at the back of the barn. There's more than one crate there. This is going to take a while.

"Reporter."

I jump as Carole startles me with my 'name.' She shimmies a little closer to me. I must look nervous because Carole gives me a sweet smile and says...

"Please dear, don't look so worried. I just wanted some alone time with you."

I smile and nod understandingly as I relax a little.

"I couldn't help but notice," Carole begins, "that you looked confused, no — baffled, by some parts of our story. You seemed *surprised* that we, the animals, have feelings, and express them."

She's right! I was puzzled. Actually, I've been confused all throughout the day as I heard the animals' stories. I need some time by myself to go over some of these stories, sort them out a bit, especially since they've all been filled with all kinds of emotions.

"Let me tell you about an excellent book, please write this down in your notes dear. It's titled, *How Animals Grieve* by Barbara J. King. She is such a wonderful author," Carole smiles affectionately. "She really understands us animals."

She waits for me to write this information down in my notebook. I look up and she continues.

"*How Animals Grieve* was discussed at our last book club meeting. Enzo reads a book on a topic that usually interests all us ladies. We meet on the first Friday of every month for a lecture at the east wing of the barn. We have a discussion and, of course," she awkwardly air quotes, 'light refreshments.'"

Oh wow, I'm impressed! Hmmm, I wonder what she means by "light refreshments."

"Carole dear," Rudy calls out. "I'll be there soon."

"Take your time Rudy, we're fine," Carole smiles, giving me a dramatic eye-roll.

"Enzo's main concern," she explains, "is that human folks can't comprehend how animals *feel* — which is understandable. Observe us Reporter, and watch your pets. Animals are a lot more complex than many human folk give us credit for having. Human folk often underestimate our emotional and our cognitive abilities. We are intelligent planners," Carole says as she waves her hoof around at Tori's elaborate decorating. "We have friends as well as beings we don't get along with — just as people do. We go out of our way to be with our special companions — just as people do. We even try to

help them the best we can if they are in danger —
just as people do. However, can human folk
comprehend how we must feel when our suckling
babies are ripped from our breasts? Can human folk
imagine how we feel when we hear the screams of
our beloved companions being slaughtered?"

I lower my head slightly as my eyes fill up. I
don't think I want to hear this now. I can only
imagine. No, no, I can't, and, I don't want to. Carole
continues while patting me on the shoulder saying.

"Reporter, I'm not telling you these things to
upset you. You are in a great position to help us
animals right now in your life. Write this all down,
okay?" She points at my notebook with her snout.

I nod, wipe my eyes and continue taking notes
— as I'm told to do.

"We *feel*, Reporter. We might mourn unlike
human folk, but even members of your species
grieve differently from each other, right? Think about
it: some humans openly cry, while others grieve
privately. Some never get over losing their spouse or
special companion, while others try to meet someone
new right away. Just because animals grieve
differently than human folk, Reporter, doesn't mean
we grieve *less*."

We hear Rudy and Tori coming back to us. I quickly blow my nose and wipe my eyes.

"You know," Carole says leaning closer to me whispering, "I want you to think about this Reporter, the main message of our discussion that night was: 'Where there is grief, there must have been...love.'"

PANIC AT THE FARM

I help Tori and Carole straighten up the last of the arts and crafts scraps into the craft box. Self-appointed Rudy strolls around inspecting everything so it meets his satisfaction. These pigs are very orderly and clean. Right then I hear commotion outside the door and —

SQUEAK!

"TORI!!"

Tori swings around. "It's Hanky, Liz, and Tiny Tina, the pigs and Mandy the goat and her kid, Emma?! What are they doing here?"

How cute! In walk three little pigs (Ha-Ha!). They are busy poking, pushing, and giggling as they toddle into the barn. Mandy, the mama goat, patiently corrals her daughter and the piglets together. Her troubled eyes look as though she is anxious to speak with Tori. This is turning out to be the most exciting "bump-on-the-head" day I've ever had in my life!

"Wow!" Tori smiles. "This place is starting to be as busy as Times Square — and I should know. What's the matter, sweeties? Why are you so upset?" Tori asks, putting down the flowers and giving her full attention to her new guests.

"Did you hear that big "Ba-BOOM" noise a little while ago?" squeals Liz.

"No, it was a "Ga-BOOM!" corrects Hanky.

"NOOOOO, it was more like a "BOOM-BOOM!-GA-BOOM!" screams Tiny Tina, who jumps to emphasize each word.

They're so cute, I wanna eat them up – NO! I cover my mouth. I can't believe I thought that. I didn't mean that – literally!

"Settle down! You three pigs *cannot* all talk at once. You're all talking *hogwash* — oops, sorry. Mandy, can you please tell me what's going on?"

Mandy is very pretty with her long, curly hair. She clearly loves her kid, Emma, and the young pigs. Could she possibly be the farm's "nanny" goat?

"Absolutely, Tori, but first," Mandy turns to the pigs, "can you three piggies do me a great big favor, and take Emma outside right now, please? Go for a walk — but not too far. It's such a nice day, and she needs some exercise." Mandy smiles and says to Tori, "It certainly does take a farm to raise the kids these days!" She lovingly nudges them out. "Thank you so much, my dear piggies, and keep a watchful eye on her for me!" Then in a serious tone she adds,

"Emma, be a good girl." Mandy turns to Tori whispering, "Let's wait, Tori, until the children leave."

I feel a little uncomfortable. Should I leave? Is this a private conversation? Tori gives me a look and motions with her head to the bench. Okay, I'm included! I sit down on the bench and look out the window. I feel somewhat honored; I get to stay with "the adults."

"Mandy, what's going on? The piglets and Emma are out of earshot now."

"There's been an accident, Tori," Mandy says solemnly. "There were a few loud bangs. I'm not exactly sure. Joey-the-goat told me he was speaking with Farmer Harry. He said to tell you that ...," she stops and looks around to make sure no one can hear, "I think someone has been... SHOT!"

Oh-my, oh-my, OH-MY!!

"OH my goodness," Tori gasps, covering her mouth with her hoof. "Miss Honey and Romeo were outside the gates of the Animal Haven ... and ...! She should NOT have gone — it's only a couple of weeks before Thanksgiving, and Miss Honey being a turkey and all ...," she shakes her head and begins to pace nervously.

"It's not safe! NOT SAFE! Romeo had a feeling, too. He warned her not to go. Oh my poor dears...

GUNSHOTS!?" Tori freezes, suddenly looking worried. "We have to prepare for a farm lockdown!" she says firmly. "It's still not safe out there!"

With one quick swoop of her hoof, all the remaining craft materials fly untidily into the box. She quickly closes it and kicks it under the table; she's now ready to take charge!

Carole and Rudy, who were sitting quietly listening to this conversation, glance nervously at each other. They bolt into action when they hear the words "farm lockdown" by instantly going to their pre-assigned stations and are preparing for all the animals to arrive.

I jump up, and then I sit down again. Then I jump up and run around a little. WHO would do this? Who would go out and kill a turkey before Thanksgiving? Oh, that's a stupid question — but not Miss Honey, my new best friend!

"First thing's first. Mandy, quickly, go tell the three little pigs and Emma to get back in here immediately, and bring in any other animal you see." Tori then adds, "Don't tell them what's going on. I don't want to start a big co-MOO-tion until we have facts." She thinks for a moment, "Tell them we are having a pre-feast meeting. Yeah, that sounds good."

I jump to my feet as she turns to me and says, "Reporter, dear, you stay where you are, and would you stop hopping up and down like a bunny! The animals don't know you yet and, sorry, but I don't want you frightening them — nothing personal."

Oops, she noticed me panicking. How sweet, did she call me "dear?" I'll sit here and make goofy faces at the baby animals. That'll keep me busy, I can do that!

Tori confidently stands at the barn door and says, "Thank you both, Carole and Rudy, for being here. I'm going to run down to the pond to give Danny the go-ahead for the warning honk. Every animal should be in the barn within ten minutes," she says, wiping a nervous sweat from her brow. "Carole, find Peter, Mall, and Merry...have them play something SOO-thing. It'll keep Romeo's hens from getting their feathers all ruffled. And Rudy, please keep order until I get back."

Tori storms out of the barn as I watch from the barn window; she hurries towards the pond to Danny, who is still on lifeguard duty closely watching the afternoon bathers. I can see Danny's startled reaction as Tori tells him the news. Then it looks as if Danny is calming Tori. He has his wing around her lower neck. It amazes me how everyone cares for each other here.

Poor Tori looks so upset, I wish I could do more than sit and pet baby animals. The animals all start filing in. I've never felt more out of place in my life. My heart breaks when I think of my new dear friend, Miss Honey. Has it only been a few hours since I first met her? I sneak another peek out the window again and see Tori heading towards the pastures. She is such a big cow, I am surprised that she can move that fast!

Tori needs to find her friends Cheyenne and Charlee. After a few deep breathing exercises that she has learned in yoga classes, she manages to relax herself, then calmly walks to the fields to find her friends. 'I have to slow down,' she thinks, 'when the other animals hear the emergency honk, then see me running, they might become frantic. Where are my 'sistas'? They've helped me with so much in the past. It's comforting how we've learned to love and depend on each other so much. I'm blessed that we're one big, happy family.' She tries to look as natural as possible, but as soon as she sees them, she breaks down and sobs like a calf. "Ohhhhhh girls, come quickly! There's been an accident, come back to the barn — immediately."

Cheyenne and Charlee look at each other in silence. Even though they want to know why their dear friend is so upset, they're too afraid to ask Tori anything. They don't really want to know; they're terrified. They've never seen her like this before. It must be very serious.

"We're chickens," Cheyenne whispers to Charlee.

Charlee shamefully shakes her head, "No, we're worse. The chickens would say and do something. We're like a lot of people. We know something is wrong, but we're too afraid to ask for information or even do anything about it once we know."

"**HONKKK HONKKK!**" Danny's emergency honk echoes through the farm. Cheyenne and Charlee jump in a panic. They immediately imagine the worst: Animal Haven is closing, and all the animals are going back to the slaughterhouse - NOW!

BACK AT THE BARN

You could probably hear an egg being laid after Danny honked his emergency honk. All the animals' 'baas,' 'moos,' 'honks,' and 'oinks' are immediately silenced. They feel something is horribly wrong.

Romeo's wives all look worried. A few of them wipe their eyes with one wing while protecting their chicks with the other. Some are nervously biting the tips of their wings.

I hold the door open as Peter, Mall, and Merry strut in calmly. They have that New York cool about them as they professionally set up their musical equipment. Huh! Where did they get that? That's nice stuff they have there.

Mandy is so very sweet. She answers questions while calming everyone in a very motherly way. Uh -oh, here comes Tori and her friends. Mandy immediately walks over to the cows.

"Tori, most of the animals have arrived," Mandy explains quietly. "Many were frightened when they heard Danny's 'emergency honk,' but I told them that you had an announcement about the party. I don't think they believe it though. Peter, Mall, and Merry are setting up to play. I suggested they start with something 'festive.' Is that appropriate?"

"Thank you so much, Mandy. That's fine. Just try to keep everyone relaxed. We should be getting word soon. I'll start in a few minutes."

Peter and Mall tune up while Merry, the chick, adjusts her gold sequined headpiece, embellished with bright yellow feathers. They all nod to each other signaling that they're ready. Merry tests the microphone by tapping it with her wing a few times before she begins. "Good afternoon, friends. Peter, Mall, and I would like you all to settle down until the rest of our companions join us. Please make yourselves comfortable as we play 'Stand by Me.'

Ready? And a one, and a two, and a…

When the night has come
And the barn is dark
And the moon is the only light we'll see
Oh I won't be afraid, no I won't be afraid
Just as long as you stand, stand by me
So Farmer Harry, stand by me, oh oh oh stand by me
Ooh stand, stand by me, stand by me"

They're amazing! I start dancing with the kids and a few lambs that were sitting by my feet. Gee,

I'm having a great time, but then I think about Miss Honey! My heart breaks for what might have happened to her today.

I glance over at Tori. It looks as if she's been crying. She shakes her tears off as I overhear bits and pieces of her conversation with Danny.

"Danny, how are the hens?" Tori asks.

"Tori, come here away from the ladies, over here, we need to speak." He leads her with his wing away from the crowd. "First of all, the chickens are understandably shaken, but they're calm enough for now. Also, I heard from Farmer Harry that...

I'm eavesdropping inconspicuously (I think) but right then the goats come in and start making noise before they are seated. Huh? What did Danny say? 'Farmer Harry is ...what? These goats are such a rowdy bunch! I try to get a little closer to hear without trying to appear to be too obvious.

"...Romeo is still missing," Danny says. "Farmer Harry wants you to make an announcement on the loss of our friend. He's going out to look for Romeo now. Also, Farmer Harry received a phone call about another farm rescue going on soon. I'm not sure when, but it sounds like a big one. It sounds like our Animal Haven family will be growing in a day or two. I'll stay with Romeo's wives."

"Danny, you're a dear."

"Tori, no, I'm a duck." Danny grins with a wink. "Will you be okay Tori to, umm… make the announcement?"

Tori wipes her eyes, and nods.

"And we have a special request from Joey, for Donna the sheep," Peter says, as Mall and Merry get ready for another song.

And ewe light up my life. Ewe give me oats, to carry on.
Ewe light up my days And fill my nights…"

"AHEM," Tori clears her throat loudly as she waves to the band to get their attention.

"Thank you everyone," Merry says. "Now if you would kindly be seated, I see that our dear Tori is ready to speak."

"Let's put our hooves and wings together for Peter, Mall, and Merry. Aren't they great?" Tori claps her hooves nodding at the musical trio. She waits until there's silence; all eyes are on her.

"First, I know rumors have been flying around the farm, so I'll get right to the point because I do have some very, very sad news. This morning," Tori pauses, "Miss Honey went outside Animal Haven for fresh clover for the Thanks-Living feast and, I'm sorry to inform you," she pauses for a moment before continuing, takes a deep breath, and says, "that she's been shot. Miss Honey was ... killed." Tori barely manages to get the last few words out before she breaks down crying.

Gasps and screams fill the barn before the crying begins. Carole, Cheyenne and Charlee run over to Tori, hugging and comforting her as they wipe their own tears off their faces.

I put my face down and cry with the rest of them. Miss Honey! My first turkey friend, the poor thing — she was so sweet. Then I notice a tiny goat staring at me closely. It's Jack-Lucas, the little goat with the prosthetic leg! I quickly wipe my eyes. He makes a silly face at me and says:

"Hi lady, don't be sad. My name is Jack-Lucas! What's yours?"

He is so tiny and has such a squeaky voice. I immediately fall in love him! I cradle his little head in my hands; the warmth from his breath is so comforting. He melts into my arms as I give him a hug. Oh, how I needed that! I look into his blue eyes. I want to say so much to him: how proud I am for his strength; how his story broke my heart while giving me encouragement to go on; how he renewed my

223

soul today — but I can't tell him anything. He came over to make me feel better! He must have been watching me the entire time, and he's trying to cheer me up! How sweet is that? I give him another hug and tickle his chin. He licks my face. Awww. I just got a tiny goat kiss! He trots away as the chickens begin to sob loudly.

"And where's our Romeo?" Janet cries from the crowd, "What happened to him?"

"To be honest with you, Janet, I don't know," Tori sadly admits. "Sometime this morning, Romeo learned that Miss Honey went out alone. He became so worried that he went out to look for her. Romeo is now missing."

Janet sits down, covering her face with both her wings. "It's all my fault," she sobs as the wives try to console her. "I was the one who told him that Miss Honey wasn't safe."

"There's no word on Romeo, Janet. I'm sure he's fine …he was — IS, umm…has always been very careful. Danny has informed me that Farmer Harry went out to search for him," Tori further explains. "He is also looking for the person responsible for Miss Honey's death. But, as I'm sure you all understand, Miss Honey was outside of our protected haven." She shakes her head trying to make sense of it all.

"Weeks before Thanksgiving is *not* a safe time of the year for a turkey to be alone in the forest. I understand that this is *not* a comfort, but sadly, a fact. Right now, we all have to think good thoughts about Romeo," she says forcing a smile. "And let's rejoice in the good, happy life that Miss Honey had with us here. We all know that Miss Honey would not have wanted any of us to be sad."

MISS HONEY'S STORY

Tori slumps onto an oversized pile of hay in the middle of the dance floor. She looks emotionally exhausted. She pounds the mound with her hooves to make it more comfortable — and to relieve some of her tension. She closes her eyes, inhales deeply, and exhales slowly. She blinks and looks around at all her friends watching her.

"Let me tell you all a little story about Miss Honey." The little ones start gathering around her as if it's 'story time.' "She was a very private turkey and once confided in me about her mysterious past. I'm sure she wouldn't have minded if I shared her story with all of you — her family."

Now the other animals start coming over to listen.

"She's named 'Miss Honey' because of the golden colored feathers on her breast and because she is," Tori pauses, and then corrects herself, "*was* a very sweet and lovable turkey. She and a bunch of chickens arrived at the farm about eight years ago. They were rescued after being discovered wandering around Harlem, N.Y. That's probably why she's been particularly close to you chickens — a kinship or a 'chick-kinship,' she would call it," Tori smiles sweetly at all of Romeo's wives. "Presumably, they were on their way to a slaughterhouse. Miss Honey joked that her gift of gab saved their lives that day. She's always been on the *beaky* side."

BRRRAAAPP!

Tori looks at me to apologize. I shake my head as I wave my hand to say forget about it (and to clear the air around me a little). We smile at each other as if we're sharing a private secret, she continues...

"Miss Honey told me that she and the chickens started a riot on the truck, but before it caused too much of a hullabaloo," she chuckles as she wipes a tear, "and ha-ha, yes she did use the word, '*hullabaloo*,' they dropped the rowdy group off right there in the street. However, on the other hoof, the truck was probably over crowded to begin with."

Everyone is now settled down listening to Tori, it's as if we are having a memorial, to honor their — our friend.

"Actually, ten more chickens and a bunch or a rafter of turkeys were freed. Unfortunately, a few got hit by cars, and some were taken in as 'pets' by people in the neighborhood," she shakes her head in disgust. "The survivors hid near some garbage cans for a few days. Miss Honey was nothing but skin and bones when they found her. She's always been so chipper and positive, considering she is in constant pain from her disabilities. Her slight lisp, which I am sure you've noticed, was caused when her beak was clipped. Her limp was due to the persistent pain of having the tips of her toes removed."

"But why, and who would mutilate our Miss Honey?" asks Hanky, one of the three little pigs. "She was such a good bird. She would never hurt anyone!"

"The workers at the slaughterhouse did that, of course!"

"Why do they eat turkeys on Thanksgiving, Tori?"

"That's a great question, Rudy. Actually, I was getting to that topic shortly."

That IS a good question. You eat turkey on Thanksgiving because...everyone has to. Isn't it ... some kind of dietary American law or something?

"Enzo, maybe you can explain." Tori puts her hoof up to her eyes scanning the crowd, she smiles when she sees him.

ENZO! I jump up and swing around as if I'm going to see a rock star. I've been hearing about him all day. Maybe he can help me find, I mean, get my voice back. Maybe he can explain my "condition." I didn't notice a man in the room. Where is he? Where is…?

Right then an enormous pig struggles to stand up. Is *that* Enzo? But, he's a pig! He's the one that … reads the paper? *He*, started a book club? I sink back down into my chair, feeling hopeless. Now what am I going to do? What about Farmer Harry, maybe he's here! I stretch my neck looking all around the barn, nope, just the animals and me. Then Enzo begins to speak, and I get a better look at him. I'm speechless (like that matters), my goodness, he has to be what…over 1,000 pounds? I've never been good at guessing a pig's weight (not that I've ever had the opportunity before). He's wearing glasses, an olive colored, zip-up cardigan and — is he really reading from a book? He seems to be quite comfortable in his "know-it-all, go-to" status — not pompous at all. Very cool!

"I'd like to begin with a thought," Enzo says slowly, carefully articulating each word. "Life is a journey, and as long as you live it, you should experience all its wonders and its joy. I truly believe that this is how Miss Honey led her life – to the fullest."

Everyone nods in agreement. Some of the animals begin to clap as they stand.

"Now about Thanksgiving," Enzo begins, "Thanksgiving originally began in this country in 1621. It was a day to give thanks with family and friends — almost like what we do here, but we only eat vegetables." He flips ahead a few pages in his book. "Many years ago, in addition to vegetables, they also ate many different types of animals, including turkeys. Then in the 18th century, due to the abundance of turkeys in the forests, it became a tradition to eat primarily their flesh. There aren't too many wild turkeys living out there now, so the people have places called 'factory farms' for turkeys to be 'created' faster, bigger— but," he looks apologetically at the turkeys, "definitely not more humanely.

"Today's factory turkeys are genetically manipulated so the turkeys grow bigger breasts. I heard that is what most human folk like best to eat. These bigger-breasted birds are so bulky that they cannot reproduce naturally. So the people at the factory farms have to…"

Everyone gasps and covers their mouths — it's quite an awkward moment, especially with the younger animals present.

"THANK YOU, Enzo!" Tori interrupts him loudly. "And without embarrassing our turkeys here any further— we'll leave it at that."

Enzo puts his hoof up in an apology; he adjusts his glasses and says, "Tori, if I may, I'd also like to add a saying from a book about a great man that I read recently. His name was Gandhi."

Tori nods.

"Gandhi said, 'The greatness of a nation can be judged by the way its animals are treated.' All animals — not just the cute and cuddly ones you people keep at home called 'pets.' I won't go into the 'what goes around, comes around' of karma, right now," Enzo says, shaking his head, "but it's not going to be a pleasurable experience for human folk. I also strongly hope that if people only knew the wretched lives and horrific deaths that we animals who are raised for their food often endure, perhaps they could change and become more compassionate regarding their consumption of our flesh."

"Thank you again, Enzo. Yes, I agree, we can only hope."

That is so very true. People have to be informed of what is going on, and then there shouldn't be an excuse for their ignorance — no more turning a blind eye, covering a mute mouth, or having deaf ears.

I see a huge cow stand up in the crowd and begin to speak...

231

"Tori, how many turkeys are killed each year before Thanksgiving?"

"Cheyenne, it is estimated about 45 million turkeys are killed *just* for Thanksgiving every year in North America."

Ohhh! That's Cheyenne! I know her story. What?! Did she just say 45 *MILLION* turkeys!'

"If only human folk realized how sweet-natured turkeys really are," Danny interrupts, "and if only they got a chance to meet one, like we know — knew — our gal, Miss Honey."

Tori nods in agreement, "I know Danny, turkeys' personalities, their temperaments, are very similar to cats and dogs who are adored and pampered by human folk.

"Here, on the farm, turkeys build nests. They care for their poults — their baby turkeys. They love taking dust baths and roosting in trees. At the factories, their lives are very different. The babies, hatched in incubators, never know the warmth of their mother's love, and yes, mama turkeys love their babies! When they are a few weeks old, they are moved to their new, overcrowded, dark, and filthy homes in the factory farms."

"I once had a nightmare like that!" squeals Hanky as he tries to hide behind Mandy.

"Yes, their lives do sound like nightmares — living nightmares! There is so much stress for our friends that some stop eating and simply die. The others are drugged with arsenic and antibiotics and are genetically manipulated to grow as large and as fast as possible."

"Is arsenic, and all those antibiotics, healthy for people?" Hanky asks, peeking out from behind Mandy.

Enzo snorts as he slowly gets up. All eyes are on him again. It's amazing how his presence and wisdom command immediate respect. "Of course not, they're harmful, but the people don't know. Most don't want to know!" he answers angrily.

"Also, if you compared a newly born, seven pound human baby who was given the same drugs that turkeys are given," Enzo refers to his notes again and continues, "he would be 1,500 pounds when he turned 18 *months* old! This large size certainly wouldn't be healthy for a human baby, just as it isn't healthy for a turkey."

What! Imagine a huge baby with stuffing and some cranberry sauce and…? I'm beginning to gag again. STOP! That's sick. I force myself to stop thinking and write it down — I have to write it all down.

233

I'm distracted as I see Joey-the-goat slowly open the barn door. Hmmm, where's he going? He's leaving the barn and...

"...many die of organ failure or heart attacks before they are even six months old," Enzo continues. "When one turkey sees his friend convulsing from a heart attack, he can also have a heart attack just from the stress!

"Turkeys, all birds actually, have no federal legal protection to help them. Since we have so many children here in the barn with us today, I will not describe what happens once the birds reach the slaughterhouse. I will say that the only thing turkeys *are* thankful for on Thanksgiving is if they get a fast and painless death, which many of them don't receive."

I didn't know that! No one thinks of this on Thanksgiving as you sit down to eat.

"What else can people eat on Thanksgiving if there is no turkey?" Mandy asks.

Another good question! I start a clean page in my notebook and title it, 'New Foods to Eat on Thanksgiving.'

"There are plenty of other delicious foods out there! It's called 'empathetic eating' or 'compassionate choices,'" Enzo says. "There are thousands of different vegetables and beans in the world. Sadly, many people think they *need* to eat meat. There are also meat alternatives; food that tastes like meat, looks like meat, actually, it cooks much faster than meat, but it is not made from us at all. As for the holidays or especially on Thanksgiving, some vegetarians and vegans often eat 'Tofurky™.'"

Little Emma jumps up and down pulling on her momma Mandy's curly hair. "Tofurky™! What kind of animal is that?! Can I play with a Tofurky™ here on the farm Mama? I'm a good girl. I like making new friends!"

"Ha-ha, no baby Emma," Tori says, "but that's a very cute thought. No, we don't have any Tofurkys™ running around here on at Animal Haven because they aren't animals.

"That's Enzo's point, dear," she explains. "Human folk do *not* have to eat animals for nourishment or to be healthy. In fact, they would actually be healthier if they didn't eat meat at all! It's really a win-win choice!

"Tofurky™ and other meat alternatives are a vegetarian protein, usually made from a wheat protein or tofu, which is a soybean protein. Human folk can make stuffing with grains and breadcrumbs flavored with vegetable Tofurky™ during the holidays but not as many as those who choose to eat actual turkey meat. The supply and demand for turkey, and all meat, would decline if more human folk would stop eating us, I mean meat, altogether, or even just one or two days a week. Why not have a 'National Meatless Monday?'"

The other animals and I agree on this idea at once by shaking our heads and applauding. Why NOT have a 'National Meatless Monday'? What a great beginning!

"Actually," Enzo stands up clearing his throat, "Meatless Monday is already a *global* concept." He pulls out a small notebook from his cardigan and begins. "It was started in this country during World War I by Herbert Hoover, who at the time was the head of the Food Administration as well as the American Relief Association, during Woodrow Wilson's presidency. This campaign first began in order to aid the war effort." He looks around the room nodding. "The notion returned with the onset of World War II to ration meat along with other items such as sugar and gasoline. It somehow lost its enthusiasm when times were good again." Enzo frowns, adjusting his glasses. "The millennium, however, revived this old idea. Back in 2003, a *new*, so to speak, 'Meatless Monday' campaign was endorsed by the Center of Livable Future. Their goal was to reduce meat consumption by 15% for personal health reasons, as well as the health of our planet. In 2009, our friend Paul McCartney, who was one of the Beatles, started a meat-free Monday campaign in the United Kingdom. Many other European countries have also adopted this movement to reduce climate change. In Belgium, it is referred to as 'Veggie Day,'" he adds with a chuckle.

I don't remember ever hearing about this before. I suppose much information is missed if one's head is in the sand. This would be a wonderful school project – as a learning project of course. The students could co-ordinate campaigns, pledges, and bulletin boards to keep track of all the animals that are saved. Students can write menus, and research healthy and more compassionate food choices. I write "Meatless Mondays" in my notebook and underline it – twice!

Rudy stands up, "Enzo, I have a question for you. Is this new?" He blinks to clear his mind. "With all this animal advocacy interest going on, why hasn't anyone ever thought of us as having feelings, or as beings, sooner? Why hasn't anything ever really been done?"

Enzo nods flipping through his notebook again, thinking, "Excellent question, Rudy. Excellent! Meat is a business, Rudy. Many people would lose large amounts of money, and many jobs would be lost if the human folk were made aware of, not only the health concerns, but also the morality of the whole situation. I want to read to you all what a 17th century British philosopher, Jeremy Bentham, argued." He lowers his glasses that were on the top of his eyebrows, *"It may come one day to be recognized, that the number of legs, the villosity of the skin, or the termination of the os sacrum, are reasons equally insufficient for abandoning a sensitive being to the same fate. What else is it that should trace the insuperable line? Is it the faculty of reason, or perhaps, the faculty for discourse? The question is not, Can they reason? nor, Can they talk? but, Can they suffer? Why should the law refuse its protection to any sensitive being? The time will come when humanity will extend its mantle over everything which breathes. "*

Everyone applauds.

Carole shyly stands up, nervously smiling at Enzo and says, "Tori, two questions. First, what is the difference between vegetarians and *vagans,* and also, do you know any famous people who don't eat meat?"

Carole smiles at me, and I give her a little wave. She blows a kiss at me. Awww! I blow one right back at her! I pet my first pig today, and she loves me — oh yes she does!

"Very good question, Carole," Tori nods. "I was detailing the differences between the two to Reporter earlier today. For those of you here who don't know, I'd like explain the dietary choices of a vegetarian and a vegan. And, Carole..." Tori adds shyly, "It's pronounced 'vEgan,' with a long 'e' sound.

"Anyhoo, vegans, besides not eating the flesh of an animal or a fish like a vegetarian, also don't eat anything *from* an animal either, like milk, eggs, cheese, or foods consisting of whey and casein, the milk's protein—which by the way, new research is indicating that it's carcinogenic, meaning, it causes cancer in people.

"Vegans also don't wear leather shoes, wool sweaters, or down coats, and they also don't use skin care products that have been tested on animals.

"The compassionate choice to not eat meat has been practiced by many people for many years, although it does seem to be more popular these days. And, yes, there are thousands of famous people, from all walks of life, actors, presidents, authors...who are vegetarians and or vegans. For instance, our Farmer Harry as well as, Gene Baur, who is an author and the founder of the first Animal Sanctuary, are both vegans. Mahatma Gandhi was a philosopher, and actor and talk show host Ellen Degeneres – both vegans. Many musicians such as Vic Fuentes, Brendon Urie, Christofer Drew Ingle, Billie Joe Armstrong and Andy Hurley, as well as John Lennon's wife, YoKo Ono don't eat meat. Also, Mike Tyson was a boxer. I wonder how many people asked him where he got his protein. Ha! Then there's President Bill Clinton, and Bob Barker who was the game show host on The Price is Right, and actors Betty White and Woody Harrelson ...to name just a few."

'To name just a few,' you just named a lot! Wow, this vegetarianism is very popular. Could it be the "new thing" to be?

"Everybody has their own reasons for eating more compassionately, some for the welfare of us animals, and some for their own health. Talk show host Rosie O'Donnell became a vegan because she had a heart attack.

Enzo stands up, "If people want to succeed, they should change slowly. It's a shame to say, but it's a radical life change for many people. Although, if you think about it, it's actually quite simple, but it could be difficult for some human folk because they are so accustomed to eating meat, two, three times a day. They don't know where to begin, *but* every step in the right direction helps. They should also get their family and friends involved. It's always easier to change your life with a friend." Enzo smiles as he looks around the room at his friends.

"The Department of Agriculture or the 'USDA" estimates that the average American eats 87 pounds of chicken, 66 pounds of beef, 51 pounds of pork 17 pounds of turkey, 1 pound of veal and 1 pound of lamb — yearly! That's over 200 pounds of meat per person! The United States population is 300 million people, so in order to feed all these hungry carnivores, 10 billion farm animals are slaughtered each year.

Tori interrupts and says to me, "Are you getting all this, Reporter?"

I jump up nodding my head "yes" and pick up my bag — from the bottom. All my things fall out with a loud clatter. I give everyone an apologetic nod, gather them up all my belongings and shove them back as quickly as I can and then continue writing. Suddenly, I feel that I have a huge responsibility to get this message out there. I can do it — I MUST do it!

Enzo is staring right at me, "To give you an example of the outrageousness of my numbers here Reporter. 4,750 animals were just slaughtered in the fifteen seconds it took you to straighten out your belongings.

I blush as I scrunch up my face, holding back all my heartfelt emotions and tears. I write down all this horrific information. This can't be right. It's insane! It's unbelievable. These sweet animals are all innocent beings. I have to be their voice. I have to!

Enzo clears his throat before he begins, "I've recently read that Sir Paul McCartney said, 'If slaughterhouses had glass walls, everyone would be a vegetarian.' Apparently, up until recently, what happens in a slaughterhouse has stayed in the slaughterhouse.

"And this is why I am extremely happy and excited that Reporter is with us today. I am sure many of you had the chance to tell her your story. Reporter, my dear friends, will *be their voice* — our voice, the voices of all the animals in the world. She seems to be a good, responsible person. Her sincerity will reach the hearts of many human folk, especially the young."

242

I jolt up from my writing and panic a little when I hear Enzo say my name again. I self-consciously stand up and smile — and jeez, did I just curtsy? He noticed what I was doing again and he complimented me! Did he just use the words 'happy,' 'excited' and 'good person?' I hope they don't want to hear me say something. I hold up my notebook and smile. I air quote — something. Sit down already! You're making a fool out of yourself again! A heated blush threatens as I remember my chicken dance routine from earlier today. I take a quick look around the room. I know everyone here. They're all my friends!

Then, quietly at first, but then it gets louder, they clap. Actually, Enzo starts. It's not your typical "hand clapping" sound. There are wings flapping and hooves thumping, but it is applause! I start to tear up and smile at all my friends. I want to give them all hugs. I wave and smile again, and as I'm bowing — that's when it happens. Out of nowhere, Emma the baby goat gives me a hard head-butt in the behind that makes me go flying, and I land on my knees. It sorta breaks my moment-of-fame mood. Everyone muffles a moo, quack, oink and....okay, they all laugh at me, but in a friendly 'don't-get-upset' kind of way.

"Emma!" scolds Mandy, her mom. "I'm so sorry. She's just being playful."

No, that's okay. It's fine. I understand, I baby-sit kids (ha!) myself, I try to say, but I spit, and my nose makes an odd whistling sound. I motion "forget about it" with my hand and smile as Enzo continues.

"Gandhi believed that: 'The future depends on what we do in the present and *now* is the present.' The countless people who will read Reporter's book, the children who will learn from it and hopefully, the generations of people who will think twice about their food, might get to know about us and understand that the meat on their plates once had a name, a family, and feelings. The true value in your story, Reporter, lies in the outcome of the change from your meat-eating readers.

"Can meat be made without slaughter?" Enzo asks and then shakes his head, answering his own question.

"CAN SLAUGHTER BE PAINLESS OR FEARLESS OR, HUMANE?"

All the animals stand and wave their hooves and wings, as they shout, "NO!"

"We hope our voices — the voices of billions of victims, innocent beings — will be heard!"

Rudy stands up and shouts, "THE TRUTH MUST BE TOLD!"

I feel like cheering too, but I emphatically nod in agreement and do my little fist shaking movement again – just to add a bit of drama.

Tori immediately agrees by standing up and nodding her head. "Yes, Rudy, the truth *must* be told! In addition..." she pauses for a few moments waiting for everyone to settle down again. "I would also like to make a public invitation — please write this in your book, Reporter — for everyone to come visit us at Animal Haven. Also, there are havens and animal sanctuaries around the country, but not enough. My personal favorites are, Farm Sanctuary in New York and California; Woodstock Animal Sanctuary in Woodstock, New York; there is another safe haven in that area called the Catskill Sanctuary, and a cute little place called, For the Animals, in Blairstown, New Jersey. All this information is on the Internet, and if you get a chance, you can read our stories as well as the stories of many more of our friends who the reporter didn't get a chance to meet. Tell the human folk to educate themselves and get more knowledge. Like Romeo says, 'Ignorance is bliss, but when you have knowledge, you then have a responsibility.' One person can do many things, even if it's only handing out leaflets, donating money to the farms, or just visiting us. People can also ask restaurants to serve more vegetarian meals."

"Leaflets?" So, my leaflet-guy in New York City wasn't out to get me! Could he have possibly been a vegetarian? Vegan? An animal activist?

"But Tori, what about Miss Honey? Will someone actually *eat* her for Thanksgiving?" Carole cries out. "She was our friend. We all love — loved her!"

"It's okay, Carole, I am sure Farmer Harry is trying his best to bring her back so we can bury her with the others who were also loved here at Animal Haven. Yes, Miss Honey was loved by all of us!"

Everyone nods, a few applaud, and some whisper as the barn becomes quiet — really quiet. Everyone is silently lost in their own thoughts, thinking of their dear friend Miss Honey and the possibility of her being the main meal at someone's Thanksgiving dinner until —

SQUEAK

We all jump from the noise as the barn door slowly opens. We turn to see Miss Honey and Romeo stroll in — wing-in-wing!

"A MOMENT FOR GRACE"

"ROMEO! MISS HONEY!?" Everyone seems to scream at once. A few of Romeo's wives gasp as they faint and fall off their perches.

I scream (silently) with the rest of them. Miss Honey, Romeo.... they're back! They're back?

"You are not going to believe the humdinger of a day I HAD," Miss Honey shrills as everyone crowds around them.

Tori laughs, but the tears are streaming down her cheeks, "Miss Honey, we thought you were ... ummm, not coming back!"

"For many minutes today, I didn't think I'd find my dear Honey," Romeo says, gazing at her.

"Let me tell you, I thought I was a goner for sure, but it wasn't me, it was that nice turkey, her name was Gracie," Miss Honey explains. "I was walking outside Animal Haven to get clover — by the way, look, I have it!!" She holds up a wingful of clover, waving it in the air as if it's a great trophy. "Anyway, I was talking to a beautiful, wild turkey. I hope you don't mind, but I invited her and her family to our Thanks-Living feast and..." She lets out a little gobble and pauses for a moment, confused by what she just said. "Oh, umm, never mind. Well, Gracie and I became jiffy friends. Such a good woman, and a mom she is — was, I can't believe she's going to be someone's holiday ...." Miss Honey puts her wings across her face. Romeo stands closer to her, wiping her eyes with his wing.

"Take a moment to *compooose* yourself, my dear friend," Tori says, patting her on the back. "You've been through too much today."

"I'm okay Tori, kinda in shock. Anyway, Gracie and I chatted for a while. We talked about life, her family, recipes, and about Animal Haven. She couldn't believe how nice we have it here. After we both found clover, I then went on my way. I do have to admit, I *did* go kinda far," she adds, nervously glancing at Romeo. "I was going to pick some wild flowers and ... Tori, the barn looks very beautiful by the way." Miss Honey prattles her "ohhs" and "ahhs" while smiling and looking at the decorations, and then suddenly grows very serious. "That's when I heard it," she says with a tense expression. "GA-BOOM!"

"I told you it was a 'GA-BOOM!'" squeals Hanky, jumping up and down giving Tiny Tina a push.

"Shhh let Miss Honey finish."

"Oops, sorry Tori."

"Well, when I heard the 'GA-BOOM,' my mind was in such a shemozzle, I scurried and hid under the bushes. I heard a few men talking." She continues quietly, "They didn't sound nice, but they were happy that they shot my dear friend Gracie. I didn't move. I was so afraid. My stomach started to feel so collywobbley that I had to put my wings over my beak to keep myself from gobbling! All I kept thinking was that I missed you all — you too, Reporter.

She looks directly at me, and I run over to give her a hug. What a relief, I was so worried about her!

She takes me in her wings, squeezing me, "How you doin' by the way? Ever find your voice?"

How sweet of her to ask. I motion, to avoid spitting on her, that, 'No, I don't have my voice yet.'

Meanwhile, Romeo is waiting for Miss Honey to finish talking. He drums his feathers impatiently, clears his throat, and he tries to console all of his wives.

His wives ... look at them all! I try to add the wives up but keep losing count with all the chicks running around. Twelve, thirteen, fourteen — no I counted her already.

"I missed you all so much, I waited, I don't know for a long time, and then I heard someone — my Romeo — calling my name," she gazes affectionately into his eyes. "I wanted to squawk and run to him, but I didn't know if those dangerous men were still nearby, so I *pssst* him."

"You kissed Romeo?" Danny asks, giving me his mischievous grin.

"No, I mean, not *then*, I, PSSST *to* him, so he could hear me."

"Is 'pssst' a word?" Hanky asks.

"Shhhhh. Let her continue!" Tori scolds quickly. She suddenly seems anxious to hear the rest of Miss Honey's story.

"Okay, umm … thank you," Miss Honey nods. "So, after I made a noise, I fluttered a little. That's when my hero found me!" She sighs, looking at him.

Romeo, who has been patiently waiting as Miss Honey told her story, now explodes with his response, "You know how I *do* tend to worry, my dear, and you were missing far too long. When I heard the gunshot…I knew it was a foolish thing to do, but I thought to myself, 'Be smart, and only trust your heart.' He breathes loudly, looking away, and then he begins.

The breeze softly sighing
In truth, may be lying
Be smart, Only trust your heart

Oh, no, he's singing again! Is this a Dean Martin song?

The warmth of her kisses
May teach you what bliss is

He sings as he holds Miss Honey lovingly in his wings, until she realizes that he's coming in for a big kiss — in front of everyone!

"Sweetie. Romeo!" Miss Honey shrills close to his face.

But this is a faithless lover's heart
Only trust your heart, the firelight

"SWEETIE!" Miss Honey squawks, whacking him hard on the head with her wing. "Romeo, focus dear, no gobbledygook with the singing yet. It's okay now. Canoodle me, stay calm." She stands a little straighter and self-consciously nods at all her friends. She then continues with her story as if nothing happened. "We stayed there, under the bushes, waiting to make sure it was clear. We had a very long talk, and ... Romeo, I think you wanted to tell your wives first," and then she hesitantly adds, "in a song."

Romeo, taking full advantage of the invitation to sing again, springs up and scurries over to Peter, Mall, and Merry. He whispers to them, they nod, giving each other an eye-roll, and mouth to each other: *"Dean Martin's 'Sway?'"*

What is this, a Dean Martin concert? He gathers all his wives in his wings and sings.

> *When marimba rhythms start to play*
> *Dance with me,*
> *make me sway*

He grabs a couple of his clucking hens and spins them.

> *Like a lazy ocean hugs the shore*
> *Hold me close,*
> *sway me more*

He takes the wings of a few more wives, very romantically nuzzles up close to them, and gives them each a peck on the cheek.

252

By this time, all of the couples are dancing, except for Miss Honey. She stands in the middle and seems to be having a great time dancing alone — it's an awkward flapping-of-wings-and-strutting-her-stuff dance. Romeo continues to serenade:

> *Other dancers may be on the floor*
> *Dear, but my eyes will see only you*
> > *and you*
> > *and you*
> > *and you*

> *Only you have the magic technique*
> *When we sway I go weeeeak*

Now Romeo walks over to Miss Honey and holds out his wing to ask her to dance. She giggles, shyly covering her beak with her wing, and then accepts. He looks up into her eyes as he sings:

> *I can hear the sounds of violins*
> *Long before it begins*
> *Make me thrill as only you know how*
> *Sway me smooth, sway me now*
> *You know how, Sway me smooth, sway me now*

As the music dies, he stands on his toes and passionately kisses her. He then turns to the crowd and says, "It's been a day of serendipitous events that bring me, us, to tell you what we've decided." Romeo pauses as he looks round the room stopping at his wives, and announces, "I've asked Miss Honey for her wing in marriage — and she's accepted."

The barn explodes with such a joyous noise. I stand up with all the animals and mouth my congratulations to Miss Honey and Romeo as everyone hoots and hollers. A few of the older animals, standing in the back, shake their heads with muffled, "tut, tut, tuts," but they don't actually say anything.

Romeo's hens look at each other, confused at first, then they all seem to jump up flapping, exciting their tiny chicks into chirping and dancing. They look at Miss Honey, inviting her over by opening their wings for her to join them. She smiles and moves in closer as they wrap their wings around her for a group hug.

"I know, I'm a rooster and Miss Honey is a turkey, but I'm sure you all understand — life is too short," Romeo says with a silly grin. "We've had feelings for each other for a while now, but we didn't *understand* them. After today's tragedy, I decided that I have to follow my heart. Carole and Rudy, I'm sure you both understand."

They both nod and put up their hooves in agreement.

"My heart led me to, my 17th wife, Miss Honey!" Romeo smiles and, with a wave of the wing, he introduces Miss Honey as if for the first time. "If you don't mind, I'd like the microphone please to sing one of my favorite Louis Armstrong songs."

"OH, jeez!" Danny blurts out.

"Danny, no wise *quacks*!" Tori reprimands grinning.

"What? I said, ummm … 'oh, geese!'" Danny answers, flashing his trademark grin.

"Go ahead Romeo."

"The very thought of you makes me
cock-a-doodle-do
Like a barn yard breeze on the wings of you,
And you appear in all your splendor,
My one and only turkey.

SQUEAK
"We know. We know. You have to get that door fixed," everyone says.

"Very funny everybody," Tori laughs. "Joey, where were you?"

"During the song Farmer Harry came in and '*pssst*' to me."

"See, that *is* a word!" Hanky squeals again. He covers his mouth, quickly glancing at Tori when he realizes that he's interrupting again.

"Yeah, right, and nevertheless," Joey says, looking slightly confused. "He told me to announce that he has to go on a big farm rescue alert tonight. He'll be back in a few days. Farmer Harry could be saving as many as sixty new friends that we have to prepare for when he returns."

Farmer Harry?! He was here! I missed him? I missed him! And now he's going to be gone for a "few days?" I was hoping he could help me find my voice and get me home. I can't stay here. I have my family, my friends and school to get home to, and now I have a book to write! What am I going to do? Sixty new animals — are coming here?

"Oh, my! Are they okay?!" Tori asks.

"He doesn't know. Farmer Harry said they were all discovered in a dilapidated, old barn cluttered with broken farm equipment and garbage. A beautiful mother sheep died, she's still there," Joey moans, shaking his head. "Her two babies were crying for her, trying to nudge her awake. Actually, about twenty-five sheep and baby lambs will be coming to Animal Haven."

"Mama, mama, I will be their friend. I love lambs!" Emma cries out.

"Yes, Emma, you can play with them and be their friend when they are well enough," Mandy lovingly answers.

"A goat," Joey continues, "needed to be rushed to the hospital because he has anemia and a parasite infection. Oh, these goats were in real bad shape, according to what Farmer Harry said," Joey says, sympathetically shaking his head. "Most of them have hoof rot and some might even have to lose the claws on their feet. It's a shame! The twenty chickens found in a dark barn with no food or water were nothing but skin and bones! There were also seven skinny cows trying to graze in a grassless pasture."

"We'll welcome them to our pasture of pleasures. They are going to love it here!" Tori says, wiping a tear from her eye with her tail.

"Tori, they will, but first they have to adjust emotionally and physically."

Why are some people so heartless?

"I hope they arrive by the time we have our Thanks-Living celebration tomorrow! If not, we can save leftovers for them if they come late!" Carole says, as she wipes off the platters on the table where the food will be served.

"They'll have to eat special diets for a while, Carole, and food has to be introduced to them slowly," Enzo advises. "According to my medical journal, we can't over-feed their delicate stomachs because they haven't eaten in such a long time."

Joey suddenly looks up remembering. "Oh, and Farmer Harry said we can't have the celebration tomorrow. We all have to pitch in and get ready for our new friends. There will be much to do! Farmer Harry said…"

Tori moans, "But Joey, what will we do with all the *fooood*?! It's ready!"

"And the barn looks beautiful, too." Miss Honey says, waving her wing displaying the room.

Tori looks at me, sighing. "And the flowers …? Reporter and I worked so hard on them."

"Calm down girls," Joey says, holding up a hoof, "I'm not finished. Like I was saying, Farmer Harry said we can't have our celebration tomorrow — BUT, we *can* have it today — right now!"

"YIPPPEEE!" Everyone shouts and immediately jumps up and swings into party mode.

YIPPPPEEE! I mouth in unison.

"Wait everyone," Tori says apprehensively, "before we get started…"

"Tori, what's wrong dear?" Carole asks, looking concerned.

"Nothing is wrong. Actually, everything is perfect. But can I please suggest something?" Tori asks, looking around the barn with an extra blink to her eyes. "Besides having our Thanks-Living feast right now, let's raise our wings and hooves and also rejoice in the engagement of Romeo and Miss Honey! We are all so happy that you both are alive and back home with us! It is truly a miracle — a time for a joyous celebration!"

"Yes! It's just what the farmer ordered — literally!" Danny says while smiling at everyone. "That *is* a great idea!"

With his wing, Romeo guides Miss Honey to step forward as he replies. "Thank you Tori, but first, may Miss Honey and I please say something? My Honey dear…"

"Yes, yes, thank you. My heart is still sad, ya know, for Gracie the turkey, who had her life stolen in the forest today," Miss Honey says sadly. "Can we all please just have a moment for Gracie? Also, let's think about *all* the turkeys who will be served as the main course in a few weeks on Thanksgiving? The lives of these wonderful, extraordinary turkeys were shortened so people can celebrate what *they're* thankful for, but no one ever thanks or even thinks about them."

Everyone bows their heads; some wipe their tears. It's quite an emotional few moments. Romeo starts to hum 'Kumbaya' but stops after Miss Honey nudges him shaking her head. I think about peace on earth, starting with one farm at a time. I've learned today that not only do the animals care for their own kind, but they protect their friends of another species – fascinating! It's too bad more people aren't so caring about others.

"Thank you, and can we also all please thank Reporter?" Miss Honey asks. "We are all so happy that you are here with us today. I am sure you'll do a hunky-dory of a job with your book about your visit here."

I jolt out of my thoughts when I hear my name. They all stand, and again I get the hooves 'n wings applause. Look at them all, my dear friends, the animals. I get up and give them a smile of thanks as I quickly look around for Baby Emma, expecting to get head butted again.

Miss Honey continues, "You are all my snicker-doodles. Thank you. That means so much to me."

CELEBRATIONS

Danny stands in front of the barn looking dapper in his jacket and grey fedora hat. He winces as he plucks out one of his green feathers from his behind, and then sticks it in the side of his hat. He waves his large wing to the crowd shouting, "Now my friends …we celebrate. We celebrate family, good friends, and our feast of wonderful food. We celebrate Animal Haven, Farmer Harry, our friendships with our fellow animals, Reporter, and most of all…we celebrate — our lives!"

Everyone hoots, hollers, and whistles; we are all ready for this well-deserved party.

Danny turns to the musical trio grinning, as he yells, "Hit it, Peter, Mall and Merry."

The three entertainers have been ready and are waiting. They nod to each other, Merry counts by nodding her head three times and they begin.

"Celebrate good times
come on! — Let's celebrate
Celebrate good times
come on! — Let's celebrate

There's a party going on, in the barn
a celebration to last throughout the years.
So bring your clucking
and your mooing too
We're gonna celebrate your party
with you!

I gather my belongings into my backpack, look around the barn, and smile. I bask in the thought of the warm friendships I've made today: Miss Honey, Tori, Danny, Carole, and Rudy. I think back to the beginning of my journey in the New York City subway with that mysterious leaflet-guy and my "awakening" moment with my head in the toilet in Paramus mall when I realized that animals, even though they are not human, are very similar to humans.

They are now all my friends. Although I'm accepted, I still feel uncomfortable and out of place because I am the only "non-animal" here. Maybe I'll take a walk and check out the rest of the farm while everyone is dancing. This might be my home for a few days until Farmer Harry gets back. Before I can wander off, Danny the duck waltzes over to me.

"Hey, pretty lady," he says with a wink.

Is he flirting with me? Did this duck just make a pass at me?

"Let's dance," he says, extending his wing. "You've had a stressful day. You need to flap your wings a little and loosen up your feathers. Come on and celebrate! Celebrate the new you! I see it in your eyes. You've changed. You're one of us now. We can find your voice later."

I shrug my shoulders. Why not? You don't have to ask me twice. Life is too short, right? When am I ever going to get a chance to dance with such a fine looking duck again? I nod, graciously taking Danny's wing, and he leads me to the dance floor. We begin to dance like the goats — as if no one is watching, but they all are. I can feel their eyes are on us, but I don't care. I'm having the time of my life with each and every one of my new friends!

"It's time to come together
it's up to you to
graze in your own pastures
everyone around the farm
come on
Ya-moo! Ya-moo!

Celebrate good times
come on
let's celebrate!
We're gonna have a good time tonight
let's celebrate, it's alright

Danny spins me around, laughing and singing, "It's alright!" loudly. I laugh and clap my hands to the music. He spins me around again, but this time I get a little dizzy, and the barn starts to whirl. Uh-oh, a familiar sensation takes over, and I feel myself spinning out of control. Could this be my portal? For a moment, I'm not really sure I want to go back.

I hear the animals, but they don't seem to notice me spinning. They continue having a good time talking and laughing. I then hear a loud swooshing sound in my head, and the animals' voices change to mooing, clucking, naaing, and gobbling. I begin to fall as I grab for Danny's wing for support. Where did he go? I lose my balance as I stumble, fall, and hit my head — again.

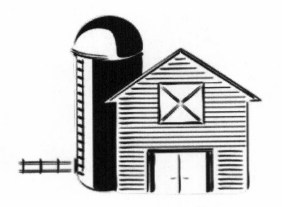

EPILOGUE

"OUCH!! &^@%!

Excuse my language." I quickly cover my mouth looking around, hoping the little ones didn't hear me. Huh, *hear me*? Did I just *say* something? Do I have my voice back? Can I speak? I try it again to be sure. "Hello? Testing, testing… YIPPEE, I can speak. I CAN speak, everyone!!" I shout.

I look around the barn. I see some of the animals: a few are eating and the others are sleeping. Did I miss the party? Did I blackout and miss the whole Thanks-Living party? Jeez, I was really looking forward to it! But I do have my voice back! I speak again — and this time a little louder I shout, "I HAVE MY VOICE BACK, EVERYONE!"

Oh, there's Charlee. I run over to her, waving to get her attention, "Hi, Charlee! We've never been properly introduced. My name is Reporter. Perhaps you've heard of me?"

Charlee looks at me, and then she turns to walk away. I gallop beside her, still trying to get her attention.

"Your 'sista' Tori, she's a good friend of mine too. She told me all about you. Your name is Cincinnati Freedom. You were a runaway from a slaughterhouse in Ohio," I rattle off.

She stops and looks at me again, seemingly giving me a few more moments of her time. "Where's Tori? How long did I black out for? How was the party? Did the new animals get here yet?" I question her quickly.

Silence. Charlee doesn't answer me. She moos disgustedly, shaking a fly off her head, and slowly walks towards the other cows in the dimly lit corner of the barn. The animals were all so friendly to me today. Tori did say that Charlee didn't like people, but that was downright rude. In a panic, I try to remember all that Tori told me about her as I shout after her, "Peter Max! I know you have the key to the city! Charlee, find Tori. Tell her I have my voice. My name is Reporter," I shout a little louder while she's still in earshot.

What's going on here?

I'm so close to tears. Why isn't she happy for me? I wonder if I did something wrong. Were my questions too personal? No, I didn't actually *ask* anything. Could she be angry with me for missing the party?

Then I see Janet eating some corn with Miss Honey's clover on it. It must be leftovers from the party. Maybe there's some extra food — I'm starving.

"Janet, yoo-hoo!" I yell, jumping up and down, "I'm over here." She looks up. I feel relieved for a moment that she's not angry with me, but then she goes back to eating. "It's Reporter, remember me? I have my voice back. Please tell Romeo that I found my voice!"

She struts away shaking her back feathers at me in an insulting way. She's been indifferent towards me all day, so I am not too surprised at her behavior.

What's going on here? I didn't *mean* to miss the party. Why is everybody treating me like this, and then it dawns on me — my voice is back, and I'm still here at the farm. Could I possibly be back to … my reality? What about my friends, all my new animal friends, don't *they* remember me?

Or, was it … all a dream?

This is just too much to understand. I slouch down on the bench and rub my head where I bumped it — twice in one day! I hum a few lines of *Celebration*, trying to remember. There's the window from where I watched Tori run to tell Danny to honk the "emergency honk." I know it. This is where I sat at the meeting during the farm lockdown. I smile, remembering how they all applauded for me. I danced with Danny at the party. That flirt winked at me. I learned the difference between being a vegetarian and a vegan, right here. This is where I decided "Meatless Monday" was such a great idea that I even underlined it twice in my notebook. My notebook!

I gasp aloud. (It's a pleasure to hear my own voice again, even if it's a raspy sound) My notebook! Where is my notebook? I need it to write my story. All their sad and adventurous stories, all the details of their lives, I wrote everything down.

Now, I'm a bit frantic. (Can you be "a bit" frantic?) Okay, I'm frenzied! My notebook is not in my backpack. It's nowhere near the bench. Think back... think back. I scan the room, trying to remember all where I've been today. Could I have left it at the pond? Did someone take it? Or ... did it even exist? I have to find it! I race around the barn kicking piles of leaves and looking behind troughs of food. I pause for a moment, catching my breath, when I spot it across the barn under some sunflowers. Oh, thank goodness, there it is!

Suddenly, an upsetting feeling creeps over me. I'm terrified to look in it — what if it's blank! That could mean that I lost my mind — then what? As I slowly walk over to it, I start to cry. This has really been such an emotional day for me — even if it might not have ever happened.

As I hesitantly bend down to pick it up, Jack-Lucas, the little goat, comes up to me. Aww...he's here to cheer me up again! I'm thrilled as he stops, looks at me in the eyes and nuzzles me with his little head. I *know* he recognizes me!

"Jack-Lucas, I'm so happy to see you," I sob. I open for my arms for a hug I very much need at the moment.

"Naa," he answers and then runs out of the barn.

"Naa?" He was so talkative earlier today and now all I get is a *Naa*!

"Jack-Lucas!" I call out after him, but it's no use, he's gone. I stare out the window to the field where he ran off. He's not coming back.

I look down at my feet to where my notebook is. I pick it up, wipe it off with the back of my sleeve, and stare at the closed book. I hesitate, the moment of truth is here and I'm so afraid to open it; it'll explain so much. Where I've been or, where I haven't been. Was it a dream? Did I lose my mind?

Maybe I won't look. Maybe I'll put it in my backpack, take it home, and then I'll decide. I can put off my "moment of truth" for as long as I want— it's my moment, I can have it when and where I choose, I think defiantly. Maybe I'll open it up next year. Yeah, that's what I'll do—next year! Maybe I'll even throw it out. Ha! I don't have to do anything. My life can go on as it was before. I don't even have to tell anyone. Who would believe me anyway? *"There's the crazy girl who the animals talk to,"* they'd say. Really, why *should* I have to do anything?

Suddenly, a "Buddha-ish" thought comes to me, *What you allow, is what will continue.* Was that Buddha or was that something I read on Facebook? I let out a deep breath as I look at my shaking hands holding the book. I have to open it. I have to face the truth — now!

I inhale the barn scents, that I'm getting accustomed to, and think of Tori. I smile, remembering all that she's accomplished in her life.

271

Such a courageous life she's lived. She's done so much and, as Tori herself said, she's "only a cow." I remember that so very clearly — she *did* say that!

A burst of bravery hits me, and I had better act on it now, before it passes. So I decide to close my eyes, count to three, and then I'll open my eyes *and* the book at the same time. (I'm real brave, huh?) Ready? "One..." (I sadly remember as I think of the last time I had my eyes closed. Romeo was telling me that awful chicken story) "Two..." (It *was* real? It *did* all happen? I had such a good laugh with Tori!) I take a deep breath opening my eyes and the book as I shout, "THREE!" Gasping and choking back more tears, I stare at the page. It's all there! My stories — their stories, their lives are all written in my notebook. It did happen! I do a little celebratory, "I-am-not-crazy-and-I-know-it dance," laughing.

My whole wonderful day *wasn't* a dream. "Yeah, I knew it!" I say a little too loudly. A mother hen looks up, and for a second I think she's going to tell me to be quiet because her chicks are sleeping, but she just turns her head.

I reread some of my notes, hoping that I might be able to mentally travel back and experience the feelings I had when I wrote them. I chuckle at my little chicken doodle captured with *poultry in motion.*

My face starts to again burn with embarrassment reading *chicken dance* with a large **X** crossing out the words. (Did I really do *that*?!) I read my list of "things I will never eat again." I flip to the page of Miss Honey's *peculiar* words; I titled it: *"Honeyisms"* - *nincompoopy, scallywag, canoodle, mollycoddle...*

I sit for a while longer, reading and reminiscing about my surreal day that I DID experience, all of my new animal friends, and all the life-changing decisions I made today. I look around one last time. I'll be back to visit, but it won't be the same. My life will never be the same again either.

I take a deep breath as I walk out of the barn. It's time to write a story; it's time to be their voice. As I gently close the squeaky barn door behind me, I hear...

BRRRAAAPP!

NOTE FROM THE AUTHOR

"Be the change you wish to see in the world." – Gandhi

Thank you so much for reading my book. As an educator, I initiated my first writing adventure not only to help myself as a new vegetarian but also as a teachable opportunity to educate my impressionable young readers - my students. I hope you enjoyed my story and meeting my friends: Miss Honey, Romeo Romero, Tori, Danny, Carole, and Rudy. I also hope you will remember my message - their message - and always carry it with you: Animals have feelings, just as we do, and we were not entrusted with the lives of these innocent beings for our consumption or misuse.

My wish for you is that you go on your own personal journey (as I have) and make more compassionate selections in your food choices. Tell

274

your family and friends — it's a more rewarding and exciting experience if you don't travel this road alone.

"What can I do?" you think, "I'm only a kid?" Tori did so much, and she was "only a cow!"

You can:

• Speak with your teachers and start a "Meatless Mondays" campaign at school. Write and post or pass out fliers. (Get permission first.)

• Ask for vegetarian options be made available in the cafeteria.

• Speak with your teachers (or better yet, find one who is already vegetarian or vegan) and ask for help in designing a bulletin board to keep track of all the animals that have been saved. This website is very helpful: http://vegetariancalculator.com/ For example: If one person does not eat any meat for one year, then 96 animals are saved! Ask your math teacher for help on these: How many animals could be saved if ten people don't eat meat for a month? Twenty for a month? Ask your classmates to cut out pictures of animals and put them on the bulletin board with the students' names. Get creative - teachers like that!

• Go food shopping with an adult and help make a meatless dinner.

- Pass out leaflets. Did you know that they are free for the asking? Hand them out to your friends and family, even at the malls or at sporting events — but please don't wave then in people's faces on the train.

- Some restaurants hand out questionnaires at the end of a meal. Write that you are a new vegetarian and, even though you love their restaurant, you would appreciate having more of a selection for vegetarians on the menu. I did that and received an email with a list of ten new vegetarian dishes to choose from WITH a 50% off coupon. (Thank you very much, Biggies in Carlstadt, New Jersey.)

- Look up "Animal Sanctuaries" and visit them. (Don't forget to bring a vegan lunch!) Talk to a cow, play with the goats, and give a pig a belly rub. It is so rewarding to be up close and personal and to be able to get a "hands on experience" with your new goal. You might even make a friend or two while you're there!

- Set reasonable goals for yourself and stick to them but also …

- Don't be so hard on yourself if you fail. If you go out with your friends and have a hamburger – so what – there's always tomorrow.

276

-     My vegan friend wanted me to add: ALWAYS bring a snack with you. It's not always easy finding a vegetarian meal, and you don't want to be tempted by hunger.

-     NEVER feel foolish for what you truly believe in.

These are just a few of many ways to start your new and exciting journey. Have fun, and keep me posted on your thoughts, your experiences, and your ideas for becoming a vegetarian. Good luck!

~Barbara

PS – People have asked me if I am vegan. I am — on most days. I call myself a "pescatarian," which means that I have fish, but I only eat shellfish once in awhile. To me, being a "vegan" is an honor, and I am not going to label myself one until I am 100%. I don't drink milk or eat eggs, but I do occasionally have a product that might contain eggs or milk. What I don't eat is: the flesh of any animal or birds. One-step at a time.

Contact info:

InnocentBeingsAuthor@gmail.com,

Facebook under: Innocent Beings (be their voice)

Twitter: BThumann-Calderaro@Innocent_Beings

REFERENCES

"Foie Gras: Delicacy of Despair | PETA.org." *People for the Ethical Treatment of Animals (PETA): The animal rights organization | PETA.org.* N.p., n.d. Web. 25 June 2012. <http://www.peta.org/issues/animals-used-for-food/foie-gras.aspx>.

"People for the Ethical Treatment of Animals (PETA): The animal rights organization | PETA.org." *People for the Ethical Treatment of Animals (PETA): The animal rights organization | PETA.org.* N.p., n.d. Web. 26 June 2012. <http://www.peta.org/>.

"Junk Food Marketing To Kids   - YouTube ." *YouTube - Broadcast Yourself.* . N.p., n.d. Web. 25 June 2012. <http://www.youtube.com/watch?v=ihu4CciAIf4>.

"The Hidden Costs of Hamburgers   - YouTube ." *YouTube - Broadcast Yourself.* . N.p., n.d. Web. 13 Aug. 2012. <http://www.youtube.com/watch?v=ut3URdEzlKQ>.

" Woodstock Farm Animal Sanctuary." *Woodstock Farm*

Animal Sanctuary. N.p., n.d. Web. 6 Aug. 2012.
<http://woodstocksanctuary.org/>.

"A Six Foot 6 Inch View on Food." *: Corn-fed Cows are Killers; Killing Us and Earth With Every Bite*. N.p., n.d. Web. 17 Oct. 2013. <http://solomon1eng103.blogspot.com/2010/06/corn-fed-cows-are-killers-killing-us.html>.

"Ag-gag Laws." *Targeting Investigations*. N.p., n.d. Web. 12 Dec. 2013. <http://www.greenisthenewred.com/blog/tag/ag-gag/Find a website by URL or keyword...>.

"Animal Facts - Pigs." *Vegan Peace*. N.p., n.d. Web. 25 June 2012. <http://www.veganpeace.com/animal_facts/Pigs.htm>.

Bohanec, Hope, and Cogan Bohanec. *The ultimate betrayal: is there happy meat?*. Bloomington, IN: iUniverse, 2013. Print.

Brown, Jenny, and Gretchen Primack. *The lucky ones: my passionate fight for farm animals*. New York: Avery, 2012. Print.

"CELEBRATION Lyrics - KOOL & THE GANG." *Song Lyrics*. N.p., n.d. Web. 26 June 2012. <http://www.elyrics.net/read/k/kool-&-the-gang-lyrics/celebration-lyrics.html>.

Campbell, T. Colin, and Thomas M. Campbell. *The China study: the most comprehensive study of nutrition ever conducted and the startling implications for diet, weight loss and long-term health*. Dallas, Tex.: BenBella Books, 2005. Print.

Castro, Jason. "GLORIA GAYNOR - I WILL SURVIVE LYRICS." *Lyrics*. N.p., n.d. Web. 25 June 2012. <http://www.metrolyrics.com/i-will-survive-lyrics-gloria-gaynor.html>.

Cowspiracy: the sustainability secret. Dir. Kip Andersen. Perf.

Kip Anderson. A.U.M Films & First Spark Media, 2014. DVD.

"DREDG - THE THOUGHT OF LOSING YOU LYRICS."
Lyrics. N.p., n.d. Web. 10 Aug. 2012.
<http://www.songlyrics.com/dredg/the-thought-of-losing-you-lyrics/>.

"Do cows pollute as much as cars?." *HowStuffWorks*. N.p., n.d.
Web. 5 Jan. 2014.
<http://science.howstuffworks.com/zoology/methane-cow.htm>.

"Famous Vegetarians - Vegan Celebrities - by HappyCow."
*Vegetarian Restaurants, Vegan Restaurant, Natural Health
Food Stores Guide by HappyCow*. N.p., n.d. Web. 26 June 2012.
<http://www.happycow.net/famous_vegetarians.html>.

"Farm Sanctuary | Watkins Glen, NY." *Farm Sanctuary |
Watkins Glen, NY*. N.p., n.d. Web. 26 June 2012.
<http://farmsanctuary.org/>.

"If Slaughterhouses Had Glass Walls | Why Vegan? | Vegan
Outreach." *Vegan Outreach | Working to End Cruelty to
Animals*. N.p., n.d. Web. 26 June 2012.
<http://www.veganoutreach.org/whyvegan/slaughterhouses.html
>.

"John Lennon - Stand By Me Lyrics." *Lyrics*. N.p., n.d. Web. 25
June 2012.
<http://www.lyrics007.com/John%20Lennon%20Lyrics/Stand%
20By%20Me%20Lyrics.html>.

July, Andrew Harris 9, and 1998 Â©. "Symbolic Meaning of
Three."   *Enkompass Default Page*   . N.p., n.d. Web. 26
June 2012.
<http://www.vic.australis.com.au/hazz/number003.html>.

King, Barbara J.. *How animals grieve*. Chicago : The University of Chicago press, 2013. Print.

License., Coolcaesar: Creative Commons. "Famous Vegans - Peter Max." *Vegan Peace.* N.p., n.d. Web. 26 June 2012. <http://www.veganpeace.com/famousvegans/profiles/peter_max .htm>.

"Meatless Monday." *Wikipedia.* Wikimedia Foundation, n.d. Web. 6 Feb. 2014. <http://en.wikipedia.org/wiki/Meatless_Monday>.

Miller, Mac. "DEBBY BOONE - YOU LIGHT UP MY LIFE LYRICS." *Lyrics.* N.p., n.d. Web. 25 June 2012. <http://www.metrolyrics.com/you-light-up-my-life-lyrics-debby-boone.html>.

"My One And Only Love Lyrics - Louis Armstrong." *Lyrics, Song Lyrics Â– LyricsFreak.com.* N.p., n.d. Web. 26 June 2012. <http://www.lyricsfreak.com/l/louis+armstrong/my+one+and+o nly+love_20268115.html>.

"Nutrition." *Vegetarian & Vegan Recipes: VegKitchen with Nava Atlas.* N.p., n.d. Web. 2 July 2012. <http://www.vegkitchen.com/vegetarian-tips/>.

"PERRY COMO lyrics - It's Impossible." *Oldies Lyrics @ OldieLyrics.com.* N.p., n.d. Web. 25 June 2012. <http://www.oldielyrics.com/lyrics/perry_como/its_impossible.h tml>.

"SWAY LYRICS - DEAN MARTIN." *Lyrics.* N.p., n.d. Web. 14 June 2013. <http://www.sing365.com/music/lyric.nsf/Sway-lyrics-Dean-Martin/E4ADE47956C7923D48256E870010FB46>.

Sanders, Anna. "Colored Chicks Raise Concerns But, After Easter, Many Face Fates Worse Than Dye | Audubon Magazine

Blog." *Audubon Magazine Blog* | . N.p., n.d. Web. 25 June 2012.
<http://magblog.audubon.org/colored-chicks-raise-concerns-after-easter-many-face-fates-worse-dye/>.

"Thanksgiving 2011 Myths and Facts." *Daily Nature and Science News and Headlines* | *National Geographic News*. N.p., n.d. Web. 26 June 2012.
<http://news.nationalgeographic.com/news/2011/11/111122-thanksgiving-2011-dinner-recipes-pilgrims-day-parade-history-facts/>.

"Turtle Island Foods, Home of the famous TofurkyÂ® and home-style tempeh." *Turtle Island Foods, Home of the famous TofurkyÂ® and home-style tempeh*. N.p., n.d. Web. 26 Feb. 2014. <http://www.tofurky.com/>.

"Vegan Outreach | Working to End Cruelty to Animals." *Vegan Outreach | Working to End Cruelty to Animals*. N.p., n.d. Web. 27 June 2012. <http://www.veganoutreach.org/>.

"Vegetarian and Vegan Information - Vegan Vs Vegetarian." *Vegetarian and Vegan Information - Vegetarians | Vegans | Vegetarian Recipes | Resources*. N.p., n.d. Web. 25 June 2012.
<http://www.vegetarianvegan.com/Vegan_Vs_Vegetarian.html>
.

"What Do Vegans Eat? | Starter Guide | Vegan Outreach." *Vegan Outreach | Working to End Cruelty to Animals*. N.p., n.d. Web. 26 June 2012.
<http://www.veganoutreach.org/guide/what_to_eat.html>.

"alphaDictionary * The 100 Funniest Words in English." *alphaDictionary * Free English Online Dictionary * Grammar * Word Fun*. N.p., n.d. Web. 22 Aug. 2012.
<http://www.alphadictionary.com/articles/100_funniest_words.h

tml>.

mistakes, amending our, and we get wisdom.. "Buddhist Quotations." *Wisdom & Fun: wise & funny quotes & jokes*. N.p., n.d. Web. 25 June 2012. <http://www.rudyh.org/buddhist-quotes-buddhism-quotations.htm>.

soundtrack. " - Some Enchanted Evening Lyrics >>." *SoundTrack Lyrics Source #1. Song Lyrics.*. N.p., n.d. Web. 25 June 2012. <http://www.stlyrics.com/lyrics/southpacific/someenchantedevening.htm>.

MLA formatting by BibMe.org.